The Adventures of

CAPTAIN GRIEF

The Adventures of

CAPTAIN GRIEF

Jack London

THE WORLD PUBLISHING COMPANY

CLEVELAND AND NEW YORK

Library of Congress Catalog Card Number: 54-5350

Original title *A Son of the Sun*
Copyright 1911 by The Curtis Publishing Company
Copyright 1912 by Doubleday, Page & Company
Copyright 1940 by Charmian K. London
Revised edition copyright 1954 by Charmian K. London,
Glen Ellen, California

HC 454

12/17/59
25383

Contents

The Adventures of

CAPTAIN GRIEF

Prologue

How many millions David Grief was worth no man in the Solomons knew, for his holdings and ventures were everywhere in the great South Pacific. From Samoa to New Guinea and even to the north of the Line his plantations were scattered. He possessed pearling concessions in the Tuamotus. Though his name did not appear, he was in truth the German company that traded in the French Marquesas. His trading stations were in strings in all the groups, and his vessels that operated them were many. He owned atolls so remote and tiny that his smallest schooners and ketches visited the solitary agents but once a year.

In Sydney, on Castlereagh Street, his offices occupied three floors. But he was rarely in those offices. He preferred always to be on the go among the islands, nosing out new investments, inspecting and shaking up old ones, and rubbing shoulders with fun and adventure in a thousand strange guises. He bought the wreck of the great steamship *Gavonne* for a song, and in salvaging it achieved the impossible and cleaned up a quarter of a million. In the Louisiades he planted the

9

first commercial rubber, and in Bora Bora he ripped out the South Sea cotton and put the islanders to work planting cacao. It was he who took the deserted island of Lallu-Ka, colonized it with Polynesians from Ontong Java Atoll, and planted four thousand acres of coconuts. And it was he who reconciled the warring chief-stocks of Tahiti and swung the great deal of the phosphate island of Hikihu.

His own vessels recruited his contract labor. They brought Santa Cruz natives to the New Hebrides, New Hebrides natives to the Banks, and the head-hunting aborigines of Malaita to the plantations of New Georgia. From Tonga to the Gilberts and on to the far Louisiades his recruiters combed the islands for labor. His keels plowed all ocean stretches. He owned three steamers on regular island runs, though he rarely elected to travel in them, preferring the wilder and more primitive way of wind and sail.

At least forty years of age, he looked no more than thirty. Yet beachcombers remembered his advent among the islands a score of years before. Unlike other white men in the tropics, he was there because he liked it. His protective skin pigmentation was excellent. He had been born to the sun. One he was in ten thousand in the matter of sun-resistance. The invisible and high-velocity light waves failed to bore into him. Other white men were pervious. The sun drove through their skins, ripping and smashing tissues and nerves, till they became sick in mind and body, tossed most of the Decalogue overboard, went to pieces, drank themselves into quick graves, or survived so savagely that war vessels were sometimes sent to curb their license.

But David Grief was a true son of the sun, and he flourished in all its ways. He merely became browner with the

passing of the years, though in the brown was the hint of
golden tint that glows in the skin of the Polynesian. Yet his
blue eyes retained their blue and the lines of his face were
those which had persisted through the centuries in his English
race. English he was in blood, yet those that thought they
knew contended he was at least American born. Unlike them,
he had not come out to the South Seas seeking hearth and
saddle of his own. In fact, he had brought hearth and saddle
with him.

His advent had been in the Tuamotus. He arrived on
board a tiny schooner yacht, master and owner, a youth questing romance and adventure along the sun-washed path of
the tropics. He also arrived in a hurricane, the giant waves
of which deposited him and yacht and all in the thick of a
coconut grove three hundred yards beyond the surf. Six
months later he was rescued by a pearling cutter. But the
sun had got into his blood. At Tahiti, instead of taking a
steamer home, he bought a schooner, outfitted her with
trade-goods and divers, and went for a cruise through the
Dangerous Archipelago.

As the golden tint burned into his face it poured molten
out of the ends of his fingers. His was the golden touch, but
he played the game, not for the gold, but for the game's sake.
It was a man's game, the rough contacts and fierce give and
take of the adventurers of his own blood and of half the
bloods of Europe and the rest of the world, and it was a
good game; but over and beyond was his love of all the other
things that go to make up a South Seas rover's life—the
smell of the reef; the infinite exquisiteness of the shoals of
living coral in the mirror-surfaced lagoons; the crashing sun-
rises of raw colors spread with lawless cunning; the palm-

tufted islets set in turquoise deeps; the tonic wine of the
trade winds; the heave and send of the orderly, crested seas;
the moving deck beneath his feet, the straining canvas overhead; the flower-garlanded, golden-glowing men and maids
of Polynesia, half children and half gods; and even the
howling savages of Melanesia—head-hunters and man-eaters.

CHAPTER 1 · *The Proud Goat of*
Aloysius Pankburn

QUICK EYE that he had for the promise of adventure, prepared always for the unexpected to leap out at him from behind the nearest coconut tree, nevertheless David Grief received no warning when he laid eyes on Aloysius Pankburn. It was on the little steamer *Berthe*. Leaving his schooner to follow, Grief had taken passage for the short run across from Raiatea to Papeete in Tahiti. When he first saw Aloysius Pankburn, that less than sober gentleman was drinking a lonely cocktail at the tiny bar between decks next to the barber shop. And when Grief left the barber's hands half an hour later, Aloysius Pankburn was still hanging over the bar, drinking by himself.

Now it is not good for man to drink alone, and Grief threw sharp scrutiny into his passing glance. He saw a well-built young man of thirty, well-featured, well-dressed, and evidently, in the world's catalogue, a gentleman. But in the faint hint of slovenliness, in the shaking, eager hand that spilled the liquor, and in the nervous, vacillating eyes, Grief read the unmistakable marks of the chronic alcoholic.

After dinner he chanced upon Pankburn again. This time it was on deck, and the young man was clinging to the rail and peering into the distance at the dim forms of a man and woman in two steamer chairs drawn closely together. Grief noted that the man's arm was around the woman's waist. Aloysius Pankburn looked on and cried.

"Nothing to weep about," Grief said genially.

Pankburn looked at him, and gushed tears of profound self-pity.

"It's hard," he sobbed. "Hard. Hard. That man's my business manager. I employ him. I pay him a good wage. And that's how he earns it."

"In that case, why don't you put a stop to it?" Grief advised.

"I can't. *She'd* shut off my whiskey. She's my trained nurse."

"Fire *her*, then, and drink your head off."

"I can't. *He's* got all my money. If I did, he wouldn't give me a nickel to buy a drink with."

This woeful possibility brought a fresh wash of tears. Grief was interested. Of all unique situations, he could never have imagined such a one as this.

"They were engaged to take care of me," Pankburn was blubbering, "to keep me away from liquor. And that's the way they do it, necking all over the ship and letting me drink myself to death. It isn't right, I tell you. It isn't right. They were sent along for the express purpose of not letting me drink, and they let me drink myself pie-eyed just as long as I leave them alone. If I complain they threaten not to let me have another drop. What can a poor devil do? My death will be on their heads, that's all. Come on down and join me."

He released his clutch on the rail and would have fallen had Grief not caught his arm. He seemed to undergo a transformation, to stiffen physically, to thrust his chin forward aggressively, and to glint harshly in his eyes.

"I won't let them kill me. They'll be sorry. I've offered them fifty thousand—later on, of course. They laughed. They don't know. But I know." He fumbled in his coat pocket and drew forth an object that flashed in the faint light. "They don't know the meaning of that. But I do." He looked at Grief with abrupt suspicion. "What do you make of it, eh? What do you make of it?"

David Grief caught a swift vision of an alcoholic degenerate putting a very loving young couple to death with a copper spike—for a copper spike was what he held in his hand, an old-fashioned ship fastening.

"My mother thinks I'm out here to get cured of the booze habit. She doesn't know. I bribed the doctor to prescribe a voyage. When we get to Papeete my manager is going to charter a schooner and away we'll sail. But they don't dream. They think it's the booze. I know. I only know. Good night, sir. I'm going to bed—unless—er—you'll join me in a nightcap. One last drink, you know."

In the week that followed at Papeete, Grief caught numerous and bizarre glimpses of Aloysius Pankburn. So did everybody else in the little island capital; for neither the beach nor Lavina's boarding house had seen anything like it in years. In midday, bareheaded, clad in swimming trunks, Aloysius Pankburn ran down the main street from Lavina's to the waterfront. He put on the gloves with a fireman from the *Berthe* in a scheduled four-round bout at the *Folies Bergère*, and was knocked out in the second round. He tried insanely to drown himself in a two-foot pool of water, dived drunkenly and splendidly from fifty feet up in the rigging of the *Mariposa* lying at the wharf, and chartered the cutter *Toerau* at more than her purchase price and was only saved by his manager's refusal financially to ratify the agreement. He bought out the old blind leper at the market, and sold breadfruit, plantains, and sweet potatoes at such cut-rates that the gendarmes were called out to break the rush of bargain-hunting natives. For that matter, three times the gendarmes arrested him for riotous behavior, and three times his manager ceased from love-making long enough to pay the fines imposed by a needy colonial administration.

Then the *Mariposa* sailed for San Francisco, and in the bridal suite were the manager and the trained nurse, fresh-married. Before departing, the manager had thoughtfully bestowed eight twenty-dollar bills on Aloysius, with the foreseen result that Aloysius awoke several days later to find himself broke and perilously near delirium tremens. Lavina, famed for her good heart even among the driftage of South Pacific rogues and scamps, nursed him around and never let it filter into his returning intelligence that there was neither manager nor money to pay his board.

It was several evenings after this that David Grief, lounging under the afterdeck awning of the *Kittiwake* and idly scanning the meager columns of the *Papeete Avant Coureur,* sat suddenly up and almost rubbed his eyes. It was unbelievable, but there it was. The Old South Seas Romance was not dead. He read:

> WANTED—*To exchange a half interest in buried treasure, worth one million dollars, for transportation for one to an unknown island in the Pacific and facilities for carrying away the loot.* Ask for FOLLY, at Lavina's.

Grief looked at his watch. It was early yet, only eight o'clock.

"Mr. Carlsen," he called in the direction of a glowing pipe. "Get the crew for the whaleboat. I'm going ashore."

The husky voice of the Norwegian mate was raised for'ard, and half a dozen strapping Rapa Islanders ceased their singing and manned the boat.

"I came to see Folly, Mr. Folly, I imagine," David Grief told Lavina.

He noted the quick interest in her eyes as she turned her head and flung a command across two open rooms to the kitchen. A few minutes later a barefoot native girl padded in and shook her head.

Lavina's disappointment was evident.

"You're aboard the *Kittiwake,* aren't you?" she said. "I'll tell him you called."

"Then it *is* a he?"

Lavina nodded. "I hope you can do something for him,

Captain Grief. He's a likable man, and he may be telling the truth; I don't know. You'll know. You're not a softhearted fool like me. Can't I mix you a cocktail?"

Back on board his schooner and dozing in a deck chair under a three-months-old magazine, David Grief was aroused by a sobbing, slubbering noise from overside. He opened his eyes. From the Chilean cruiser, a quarter-mile away, came the stroke of eight bells. It was midnight. From overside came a splash and another slubbering noise. To him it seemed half-amphibian, half the sound of a man crying to himself and querulously chanting his sorrows to the general universe.

A jump took David Grief to the low rail. Beneath, centered about the slubbering noise, was an area of agitated phosphorescence. Leaning over, he locked his hand under the armpit of a man, and with pull and heave and quick-changing grips, he drew on deck the naked form of Aloysius Pankburn.

"I didn't have a penny," Pankburn complained. "I had to swim it, and I couldn't find your gangway. It was very miserable. Pardon me. If you have a towel to put about my middle, and a good stiff drink, I'll be more myself. I'm Mr. Folly, and you're the Captain Grief, I presume, who called on me when I was out. No, I'm not drunk. Nor am I cold. This isn't shivering. Lavina allowed me only two drinks today. I'm on the edge of the horrors, that's all, and I was beginning to see things when I couldn't find the gangway. If you'll take me below I'll be very grateful. You are the only one that answered my advertisement."

He was shaking pitiably in the warm night, and down in the cabin, before he got his towel, Grief saw to it that a half-tumbler of whiskey was in his hand.

"Now fire away," Grief said, when he had got his guest into a shirt and a pair of duck trousers. "What's this advertisement of yours? I'm listening."

Pankburn looked at the whiskey bottle, but Grief shook his head.

"All right, Captain, though I tell you on whatever is left of my honor that I am not drunk—not in the least. Also, what I shall tell you is true, and I shall tell it briefly, for it is clear to me that you are a man of affairs and action. Likewise, your chemistry is good. To you alcohol has never been a million maggots gnawing at every cell of you. You've never been to hell. I am there now. I am scorching. Now listen.

"My mother is alive. She is English. I was born in Australia. I was educated at York and Yale. I am a master of arts, a doctor of philosophy, and I am no good. Furthermore, I am an alcoholic. I have been an athlete. I used to swan dive a hundred and ten feet in the clear. I hold several amateur records. I swim like a fish. I have done thirty miles in a rough sea. I have another record. I have punished more whiskey than any man of my years. I will steal a nickel from you for the price of a drink. Finally, I will tell you the million-dollar story.

"My father was an American—an Annapolis man, lieutenant on the *Suwanee*. Her captain was Paul Shirley. The *Suwanee* once coaled at an island in the Pacific which I do not care to mention, now under a protectorate which did not exist then and which shall be nameless. Ashore, behind the bar of a public house, my father saw three copper spikes—ship's spikes."

David Grief smiled quietly. "And I can tell you the name of the coaling station and of the protectorate that came afterward," he said.

"And of the three spikes?" Pankburn asked with equal quietness. "Go ahead, for they are now in my possession."

"Certainly. They were behind German Oscar's bar at Peenoo-Peenee. Johnny Black brought them there from off his schooner the night he died. He was just back from a long cruise to the westward, fishing bêche-de-mer and sandalwood trading. All the beach knows the tale."

Pankburn nodded his head. "Go on," he urged.

"It was before my time, of course," Grief explained. "I only tell what I've heard. Next came the Ecuadorian cruiser, in from the westward of all directions, and bound home. Her officers recognized the spikes. Johnny Black was dead. They got hold of his mate and logbook. Away to the westward she went. Six months after, again bound home, she dropped in at Peenoo-Peenee. She had failed, and the tale leaked out."

"When the revolutionists were marching on Guayaquil," Pankburn took it up, "the Federal officers, believing a defense of the city hopeless, salted down the government treasure chest, something like a million dollars gold, but all in English coinage, and put it on board the American schooner *Flirt*. *They* were going to run at daylight—the American captain skinned out in the middle of the night. Go on."

"It's an old story," Grief resumed. "There was no other vessel in the harbor. The Federal leaders couldn't run. They put their backs to the wall and held the city. Rohjas Salced, making a forced march from Quito, raised the siege. The revolution was broken, and the one ancient steamer that constituted the Ecuadorian navy was sent in pursuit of the *Flirt*. They caught her, between the Banks Group and the New Hebrides, hove to and flying distress signals. The captain had died the day before—blackwater fever."

"And the mate?" Pankburn challenged.

"The mate had been killed a week earlier by the natives on one of the Banks, when they sent a boat in for water. There were no navigators left. The men were put to torture. It was beyond international law. They wanted to confess, but couldn't. They told of the three spikes in the trees on the beach, but where the island was they did not know. To the westward, far to the westward, was all they knew. The tale now goes two ways. One is that they all died under the torture. The other is that the survivors were swung at the yardarm. At any rate, the Ecuadorian cruiser went home without the treasure. Johnny Black had brought the three spikes to Peenoo-Peenee, and left them at German Oscar's, but how and where *he* found them he never told."

Pankburn looked hard at the whiskey bottle.

"Just two fingers," he whimpered.

Grief considered, and poured a meager drink. Pankburn's eyes sparkled, and he took a new lease on life.

"And this is where I come in with the missing details," he said. "Johnny Black *did* tell. *He told my father*. Wrote him from Levuka, before he came on to die at Peenoo-Peenee. My father had saved his life one roughhouse night in Valparaiso. A Chinese pearler, out of Thursday Island, prospecting for new grounds to the north of New Guinea, traded for the three spikes somewhere with a native. Johnny Black bought them for the copper. He didn't dream any more than

the Chinese that they meant anything special, but coming
back he stopped for hawksbill turtle at the very beach where
you say the mate of the *Flirt* was killed. Only he wasn't
killed. The Banks Islanders held him prisoner, and he was
dying of necrosis of the jawbone, caused by an arrow wound
in the fight on the beach. Before he died he told the whole
story to Johnny Black. Johnny Black wrote my father from
Levuka. He was at the end of his rope—cancer. My father
got the spikes from German Oscar. And from my father,
last will and testament, you know, came the spikes and the
data. I have the island, the latitude and longitude of the
beach where the three spikes were nailed in the trees. The
spikes are up at Lavina's now. The latitude and longitude
are in my head. Now what do you think?"

"Fishy," was Grief's instant judgment. "Why didn't your
father go and get it himself?"

"Didn't need it. An uncle died and left him a fortune.
He retired from the navy, ran afoul of an epidemic of trained
nurses in Boston, and my mother got a divorce. Also, she
fell heir to an income of something like thirty thousand dollars, and went to live in New Zealand. I was divided between
them, half the time New Zealand, half the time United States,
until my father's death last year. Now my mother has me altogether. He left me his money—a couple of millions—but
my mother has had guardians appointed on account of the
liquor. I'm worth all kinds of money, but I can't touch a
penny save what is doled out to me. But the old man, who
had got the tip on my drinking, left me the three spikes and
the data thereunto pertaining. Did it through his lawyers,
unknown to my mother; said it beat life insurance, and that

if I had the backbone to go and get it I could drink my back teeth awash until I died. Millions in the hands of my guardians, lots of my mother's dough that'll be mine if she beats me to the crematory, another million waiting to be dug up, and in the meantime I'm cadging on Lavina for two drinks a day. It's hell, isn't it—when you consider my thirst?"

"Where's the island?"

"A long way from here."

"Name it."

"Not on your life, Captain Grief. You're making an easy half-million out of this. You will sail under my directions, and when we're well to sea and on our way I'll tell you—not before."

Grief shrugged his shoulders, dismissing the subject.

"When I've given you another drink I'll send the boat ashore with you," he said.

Pankburn was taken aback. For at least five minutes he debated with himself, then licked his lips and surrendered.

"If you promise to go, I'll tell you now."

"Of course I'm willing to go. That's why I asked you. Name the island."

Pankburn looked at the bottle.

"I'll take that drink now, Captain."

"No you won't. That drink was for you if you went ashore. If you are going to tell me the island, you must do it sober."

"Francis Island, since you insist. Bougainville named it Barbour Island."

"Off there all by its lonely in the Little Coral Sea," Grief said. "I know it. Lies between New Ireland and New Guinea. A rotten hole now, though it was all right when the *Flirt* drove in the spikes and the Chinese pearler traded for them. The steamship *Castor*, recruiting labor for the Samoan plantations, was cut off there with all hands two years ago. I knew her captain well. The Germans sent a cruiser, shelled the bush, burned half a dozen villages, killed a couple of natives and a lot of pigs, and—and that was all. The natives always were mad there, but they turned really mad forty years ago. That was when they cut off a whaler. Let me see—what was her name?"

He stepped to the bookshelf, drew out the bulky *South Pacific Directory*, and ran through its pages.

"Yes. Here it is. *Francis,* or *Barbour*," he skimmed. "Natives warlike—Melanesian. Whaleship *Western* cut off—that was her name. Shoals—points—anchorages—ah, Redscar, Owen Bay, Likikili Bay, that's more like it; deep indentation, mangrove swamps, good holding in nine fathoms when white scar in bluff bears west-southwest." Grief looked up. "That's your beach, Pankburn, I'll swear."

"Will you go?" the other demanded eagerly.

Grief nodded. "It sounds good to me. Now if the story had been of a hundred million, or some such crazy sum, I wouldn't look at it for a moment. We'll sail tomorrow, but under one consideration. You are to be absolutely under my orders."

His visitor nodded emphatically and joyously.

"And that means no drink."

"That's pretty hard," Pankburn whined.

"It's my terms. I'm enough of a doctor to see you don't come to harm. And you are to work—hard work, sailor's work. You'll stand regular watches and everything, though you eat and sleep aft with us."

"It's a deal." Pankburn put out his hand to ratify the agreement. "If it doesn't kill me," he added.

David Grief poured a generous three-fingers into the tumbler and extended it.

"Then here's your last drink. Take it."

Pankburn's hand went halfway out. With a sudden spasm of resolution, he hesitated, threw back his shoulders, and straightened up his head.

"I guess I won't," he began—then, feebly surrendering to the gnaw of desire, he reached hastily for the glass, as if in fear that it would be withdrawn.

It is a long traverse from Papeete in Tahiti to the Little Coral Sea—from 150 west longitude to 150 east longitude—as the crow flies, equivalent to a voyage across the Atlantic. But the *Kittiwake* did not go as the crow flies. David Grief's numerous interests diverted her course many times. He stopped to have a look-in at uninhabited Rose Island with an eye to colonizing and planting coconuts. Next, he paid his respects to Tui Manua of Eastern Samoa, and opened an intrigue for a share of the trade monopoly of that dying king's three islands. From Apia he carried several relief agents and a load of trade goods to the Gilberts. He peeped in at Ontong Java Atoll, inspected his plantations on Santa Isabel, and purchased lands from the salt-water chiefs of northwestern Malaita. And all along this devious way he made a man of Aloysius Pankburn.

That thirster, though he lived aft, was compelled to do the work of a common sailor. And not only did he take his wheel and lookout, and heave on sheets and tackles, but the dirtiest and most arduous tasks were appointed him. Swung aloft in a bosun's chair, he scraped the masts and slushed down. Holystoning the deck or scrubbing it with fresh limes made his back ache and developed the wasted, flabby muscles. When the *Kittiwake* lay at anchor and her copper bottom was scrubbed with coconut husks by the native crew, who dived and did it under water, Pankburn was sent down on his shift —and as many times as any on the shift.

"Look at yourself," Grief said. "You are twice the man you were when you came on board. You haven't had one drink, you didn't die, and the poison is pretty well worked out of you. It's the work. It beats trained nurses and business managers. Here, if you're thirsty. Clap your lips to this."

With several deft strokes of his heavy-backed sheath knife, Grief clipped a triangular piece of shell from the end of a husked drinking-coconut. The thin, cool liquid, slightly milky and effervescent, bubbled to the brim. With a bow, Pankburn took the natural cup, threw his head back, and held it back till the shell was empty. He drank many of these nuts each day. The steward, a New Hebrides native sixty years of age, and his assistant, a Lark Islander of eleven, saw to it that he was continually supplied.

Pankburn did not object to the hard work. He devoured work, never shirking and always beating the native sailors in jumping to obey a command. But his sufferings during the period of driving the alcohol out of his system were truly heroic. Even when the last shred of the poison was exuded, the desire, as an obsession, remained in his head. So it was, when, on his honor, he went ashore at Apia in Samoa, that he attempted to put the bars out of business by drinking up their stock in trade. And so it was, at two in the morning, that David Grief found him in front of the Tivoli, out of which he had been thrown by Charley Roberts. Aloysius, as of old, was chanting his sorrows to the stars. Also, and more concretely, he was punctuating the rhythm with cobbles of coral stone, which he flung with amazing accuracy through Charley Roberts' windows.

David Grief took him away, but not till next morning did he take him in hand. It was on the deck of the *Kittiwake*, and there was nothing kindergarten about it. Grief struck him with bare knuckles, punched him and punished him—gave him the worst thrashing he had ever received.

"For the good of your soul, Pankburn," was the way he emphasized his blows. "For the good of your mother. For the progeny that will come after. For the good of the world, and the universe, and the whole race of man yet to be. And now, to hammer the lesson home, we'll do it all over again. That, for the good of your soul; and that, for your mother's sake; and that, for the little children, undreamed of and unborn, whose mother you'll love for their sakes, and for love's sake, in the lease of manhood that will be yours when I am done with you. Come on and take your medicine. I'm not done with you yet. I've only begun. There are many other reasons which I shall now proceed to explain to you."

The sailors and the stewards and cook looked on and grinned. As for Carlsen, the mate, he was grimly in accord with the treatment his employer was administering; while Albright, the supercargo, merely played with his mustache and smiled. They were men of the sea. They lived life in the rough. And alcohol, in themselves as well as in other men, was a problem they had learned to handle in ways not taught in doctors' schools.

"Steward! A bucket of fresh water and a towel," Grief ordered, when he had finished. "Two buckets and two towels," he added, as he surveyed his own hands.

"You're a pretty one," he said to Pankburn. "You've spoiled everything. I had the poison completely out of you. And now you are fairly reeking with it. We've got to begin all over again. Mr. Albright! You know that pile of old chain on the beach at the boat landing. Find the owner, buy it, and fetch it on board. There must be a hundred and fifty fathoms of it. Pankburn! Tomorrow morning you start pounding the rust off of it. When you've done that, you'll sandpaper it. Then you'll paint it. And nothing else will you do till that chain is as smooth as new."

Aloysius Pankburn shook his head.

"I quit. Francis Island can go to hell for all of me. I'm done with your slave driving. Kindly put me ashore at once. You can't treat me this way."

"Mr. Carlsen, you will see that Mr. Pankburn remains on board."

"I'll fix you for this!" Aloysius screamed. "You can't keep me here!"

"I can give you another licking," Grief answered. "And let me tell you one thing, you besotted whelp—I'll keep on licking you as long as my knuckles hold out or until you yearn to hammer chain rust. I've taken you in hand and I'm going to make a man out of you if I have to kill you to do it. Now go below and change your clothes. Be ready to turn to with a hammer this afternoon. Mr. Albright, get that chain aboard pronto. Mr. Carlsen, send the boats ashore after it. Also, keep your eye on Pankburn. If he shows signs

of keeling over or going into the shakes, give him a nip—
a small one. He may need it after last night."

For the rest of the time the *Kittiwake* lay in Apia, Aloysius
Pankburn pounded chain rust. Ten hours a day he pounded.
And on the long stretch across to the Gilberts he still pounded.
Then came the sandpapering. One hundred and fifty fathoms is nine hundred feet, and every link of all that length
was smoothed and polished as no link ever was before. And
when the last link had received its second coat of black paint,
he declared himself.

"Come on with more dirty work," he told Grief. "I'll overhaul the other chains if you say so. And you needn't worry
about me any more. I'm not going to take another drop. I'm
going to train up. You got my goat when you beat me, but
let me tell you, you only got it temporarily. Train! I'm going
to train till I'm as hard all the way through—and clean all
the way through—as that chain is. And some day, Mr. David
Grief, somewhere, somehow, I'm going to be in such shape
that I'll lick you as you licked me. I'm going to pulp your
face till your own sailors won't know you."

Grief was jubilant.

"Now you're talking like a man," he cried. "The only
way you'll ever lick me is to become a man. And then,
maybe—"

He paused in the hope that the other would catch the suggestion. Aloysius groped for it, and, abruptly, something akin
to illumination shone in his eyes.

"And then I won't want to, you mean?"

Grief nodded.

"And that's the curse of it," Aloysius lamented. "I really believe I won't want to. I see the point. But I'm going to go right on and shape myself up just the same."

The warm, sunburn glow in Grief's face seemed to grow warmer. His hand went out.

"Pankburn, I love you right now for that."

Aloysius grasped the hand, and shook his head in sad sincerity.

"Grief," he mourned, "you've got my goat, you've got my proud goat, and you've got it permanently, I'm afraid."

On a sultry tropic day, when the last flicker of the far southeast trade was fading out and the seasonal change for the northwest monsoon was coming on, the *Kittiwake* lifted above the sea rim the jungle-clad coast of Francis Island. Grief, with compass bearings and binoculars, identified the volcano that marked Redscar, ran past Owen Bay, and lost the last of the breeze at the entrance to Likikili Bay. With the two whaleboats out and towing, and with Carlsen heaving the lead, the *Kittiwake* sluggishly entered a deep and narrow indentation. There were no beaches. The mangroves began at the water's edge, and behind them rose steep jungle, broken here and there by jagged peaks of rock. At the end of a mile, when the white scar on the bluff bore westsouthwest, the lead vindicated the *Directory*, and the anchor rumbled down in nine fathoms.

For the rest of that day and until the afternoon of the day following they remained on the *Kittiwake* and waited. No canoes appeared. There were no signs of human life. Save for the occasional splash of a fish or the screaming of cockatoos, there seemed no other life. Once, however, a huge butterfly, twelve inches from tip to tip, fluttered high over their mastheads and drifted across to the opposing jungle.

"There's no use sending a boat in to be cut up," Grief said.

Pankburn was incredulous, and volunteered to go in alone, to swim it if he couldn't borrow the dinghy.

"They haven't forgotten the German cruiser," Grief explained. "I'll wager that bush is alive with men right now. What do you think, Mr. Carlsen?"

That veteran adventurer of the islands was emphatic in his agreement.

In the late afternoon of the second day Grief ordered a whaleboat into the water. He took his place in the bow, a cigarette in his mouth and a short-fused stick of dynamite in his hand, for he was bent on shooting a mess of fish. Along the thwarts half a dozen Winchesters were placed. Albright, who took the steering sweep, had a Mauser within reach. They pulled in and along the green wall of vegetation. At times they rested on the oars in the midst of a profound silence.

"Two to one the bush is swarming with them—on a five spot," Albright whispered.

Pankburn listened a moment longer and took the bet. Five minutes later they sighted a school of mullet. The rowers held their oars. Grief touched the short fuse to his cigarette and threw the stick. So short was the fuse that the stick exploded the instant after it struck the water. And in that same instant the bush exploded into life. There were wild yells of defiance, and naked bodies leaped forward through the mangroves.

In the whaleboat every rifle was lifted. Then came the wait.

A hundred aborigines, some few armed with ancient Sniders, but the greater portion armed with tomahawks, fire-hardened spears, and bone-tipped arrows, clustered on the roots that rose out of the bay. No word was spoken. Each party watched the other across twenty feet of water. An old, one-eyed chief with a bristly face rested a Snider on his hip, the muzzle directed at Albright, who, in turn, covered him back with the Mauser. A couple of minutes of this tableau endured. The stricken fish rose to the surface or struggled half-stunned in the clear depths.

"It's all right, boys," Grief said quietly. "Put down your guns and over the side with you. Mr. Albright, toss the tobacco to that one-eyed gentleman."

While the Rapa men dived for the fish, Albright threw a bundle of trade-tobacco ashore. The one-eyed man nodded his head and writhed his features in an attempt at amiability. Weapons were lowered, bows unbent, and arrows put back in their quivers.

"They know tobacco," Grief announced, as they rowed back aboard. "We'll have visitors. You'll break out a case of tobacco, Mr. Albright, and a few trade-knives. There's a canoe now."

Old One-Eye, as befitted a chief and leader, paddled out alone, facing peril for the rest of the tribe. As Carlsen leaned over the rail to help the visitor up, he turned his head and remarked casually:

"They've dug up the money, Mr. Grief. The old man's loaded with it."

One-Eye floundered down on deck, grinning appeasingly and failing to hide the fear he had overcome but which still possessed him. He was lame of one leg, and this was accounted for by a terrible scar, inches deep, which ran down the thigh from hip to knee. No clothes he wore whatever, not even a string, but his nose, perforated in a dozen places and each perforation the setting for a carved spine of bone, bristled like a porcupine. Around his neck and hanging down on his chest was a string of gold sovereigns. His ears were hung with silver half crowns, and from the cartilage separating his nostrils depended a big English penny, tarnished and green, but unmistakable.

"Hold on, Grief," Pankburn said, with perfectly assumed carelessness. "You say they know only beads and tobacco. Very well. You follow my lead. They've found the treasure, and we've got to trade them out of it. Get the whole crew aside and lecture them that they are to be interested only in the pennies. Savvy? Gold coins must be beneath contempt, and silver coins merely tolerated. Pennies are to be the only desirable things."

Pankburn took charge of the trading. For the penny in One-Eye's nose he gave ten sticks of tobacco. Since each stick cost David Grief a cent, the bargain was manifestly unfair. But for the half crowns Pankburn gave only one stick each. The string of sovereigns he refused to consider. The more he refused, the more One-Eye insisted on a trade. At last, with an appearance of irritation and anger, and as a palpable concession, Pankburn gave two sticks for the string, which was composed of ten sovereigns.

"I take my hat off to you," Grief said to Pankburn that night at dinner. "You've reversed the scale of value. They'll figure the pennies as priceless possessions and the sovereigns as beneath price. Result: they'll hang on to the pennies and force us to trade for sovereigns. Pankburn, I drink your health! Steward!—another cup of tea for Mr. Pankburn."

Followed a golden week. From dawn till dark a row of canoes rested on their paddles two hundred feet away. This was the deadline. Rapa sailors, armed with rifles, maintained it. Only one canoe at a time was permitted alongside, and only one native at a time was permitted to come over the rail. Here, under the awning, relieving one another in hourly shifts, the four white men carried on the trade. The rate of exchange was that established by Pankburn with One-Eye. Five sovereigns fetched a stick of tobacco; a hundred sovereigns, twenty sticks. Thus, an aborigine would deposit on the table a thousand dollars in gold, and go back over the rail, hugely satisfied, with forty cents' worth of tobacco in his hand.

"Hope we've got enough tobacco to hold out," Carlsen muttered dubiously, as another case was sawed in half.

Albright laughed.

"We've got fifty cases below," he said, "and as I figure it, three cases buy a hundred thousand dollars. There was only a million dollars buried, so thirty cases ought to get it. Though, of course, we've got to allow a margin for the silver and the pennies. That Ecuadorian bunch must have salted down all the coin in sight."

Very few pennies and shillings appeared, though Pankburn continually and anxiously inquired for them. Pennies were the one thing he seemed to desire, and he made his eyes flash covetously whenever one was produced. True to his theory, the natives concluded that the gold, being of slight value, must be disposed of first. A penny, worth fifty times as much as a sovereign, was something to retain and treasure. Doubtless, in their jungle lairs, the wise old graybeards put their heads together and agreed to raise the price on pennies when the worthless gold was all worked off. Who could tell? Mayhap the strange white men could be made to give even twenty sticks for a priceless copper.

By the end of the week the trade went slack. There was only the slightest dribble of gold. An occasional penny was reluctantly disposed of for ten sticks, while several thousand dollars in silver came in.

On the morning of the eighth day no trading was done. The graybeards had matured their plan and were demanding twenty sticks for a penny. One-Eye delivered the new rate of exchange. The white men appeared to take it with great seriousness, for they stood together debating in low voices. Had One-Eye understood English he would have been enlightened.

"We've got just a little over eight hundred thousand, not counting the silver," Grief said. "And that's about all there is. The bush tribes behind have most probably got the other two hundred thousand. Return in three months, and the salt-water crowd will have traded back for it; also they will be out of tobacco by that time."

"It would be a sin to buy pennies," Albright grinned. "It goes against the thrifty grain of my trader's soul."

"There's a whiff of land breeze stirring," Grief said, looking at Pankburn. "What do you say?"

Pankburn nodded.

"Very well." Grief measured the faintness and irregularity

of the wind against his cheek. "Mr. Carlsen, heave short, and get off the gaskets. And stand by with the whaleboats to tow. This breeze is not dependable."

He picked up a part case of tobacco, containing six or seven hundred sticks, put it in One-Eye's hands, and helped that bewildered native over the rail. As the foresail went up the mast, a wail of consternation arose from the canoes lying along the deadline. And as the anchor broke out and the *Kittiwake's* head paid off in the light breeze, old One-Eye, daring the rifles leveled on him, paddled alongside and made frantic signs of his tribe's willingness to trade pennies for ten sticks.

"Steward!—a drinking nut," Pankburn called.

"It's Sydney Heads for you," Grief said. "And then what?"

"I'm coming back with you for that two hundred thousand," Pankburn answered. "In the meantime I'm going to build an island schooner. Also, I'm going to haul those guardians of mine into court to show cause why my father's money should not be turned over to me. Show cause? I'll show them cause why it should."

He swelled his biceps proudly under the thin sleeve.

"Come on! Swing out on that foreboom tackle!" Carlsen shouted from aft, where the mainsail was being winged out.

Pankburn dropped his coconut and raced for it, beating a Rapa sailor by two jumps to the hauling part.

CHAPTER 2 · *The Devils of Fuatino*

OF HIS many schooners, ketches and cutters that nosed about among the coral isles of the South Seas, David Grief loved most the *Rattler*—a yacht-like schooner of ninety tons with so swift a pair of heels that she had made herself famous in the old days, opium-smuggling from San Diego to Puget Sound, raiding the seal rookeries of the Bering Sea, and running arms in the Far East. A stench and an abomination to government officials, she had been the joy of all sailoring men and the pride of the shipwrights who built her. Even now, after forty years of driving, she was still the same old *Rattler*, forereaching in the same marvelous manner that compelled sailors to see in order to believe and that punctuated many an angry discussion with words and blows on the beaches of ports from Valparaiso to Manila Bay.

37

On this night, close-hauled, her big mainsail preposterously flattened down, her luffs pulsing emptily on the lift of each smooth swell, she was sliding an easy four knots through the water on the veriest whisper of a breeze. For an hour David Grief had been leaning on the rail at the lee fore-rigging, gazing overside at the steady phosphorescence of her gait. The faint back-draft from the headsails fanned his cheek and chest with a wine of coolness, and he was in an ecstasy of appreciation of the schooner's qualities.

"She's a beauty, Taute, a beauty," he said to the Kanaka lookout, at the same time stroking the teak of the rail with an affectionate hand.

"Ay, skipper," the Kanaka answered in the rich, big-chested tones of Polynesia. "Thirty years I know ships, but never like this. On Raiatea we call her *Fanauao*."

" 'The Dayborn,' " Grief translated the love-phrase. "Who named her so?"

About to answer, Taute peered ahead with sudden intensity. Grief joined him in the gaze.

"Land," said Taute.

"Yes; Fuatino," Grief agreed, his eyes still fixed on the spot where the star-luminous horizon was gouged by a blot of blackness. "I'll tell the captain."

The *Rattler* slid along until the loom of the island could be seen as well as sensed, until the sleepy roar of breakers and the blatting of goats could be heard, until the wind off the land was flower-drenched with perfume.

"If it wasn't a crevice, she could run the passage on a night like this," Captain Glass remarked regretfully, as he watched the wheel lashed hard down by the steersman.

The *Rattler*, run off shore a mile, had been hove to to wait until daylight before she attempted the perilous entrance to Fuatino. It was a perfect tropic night, with no hint of rain or squall. For'ard, wherever their tasks left them, the Raiatea sailors sank down to sleep on deck. Aft, the captain and mate and Grief spread their beds with similar languid unconcern. They lay on their blankets, smoking and murmuring sleepy conjectures about Mataara, the Queen of Fuatino, and about the love affair between her daughter, Naumoo, and Motuaro.

"They're certainly a romantic lot," Brown the mate, said.

"As romantic as Pilsach," Grief laughed, "and that is going some. How long ago was it, Captain, that he jumped you?"

"Eleven years," Captain Glass grunted resentfully.

"Tell me about it," Brown asked. "They say he's never left Fuatino since. Is that right?"

"Righto," the captain rumbled. "He's in love with his wife —the little hussy! Stole him from me, and he as good a sailorman as the trade has ever seen—even if he is a Dutchman."

"German," Grief corrected.

"It's all the same," was the retort. "The sea was robbed of a good man that night he went ashore and Notutu took one look at him. I reckon they looked good to each other. Before you could say boo, she'd put a wreath of some kind of white flowers on his head, and in five minutes they were off down the beach like a couple of kids, holding hands and laughing. I only hope he's finally blasted that big coral patch out of the channel. I always start a sheet or two of copper warping past."

"Go on with the story," Brown urged.

"That's all. He was finished right there. Got married that night. Never came on board again. I looked him up next day. Found him in a straw house in the bush, barelegged, all mixed up with flowers and things and playing a guitar. Looked like a bloody fool. Told me to send his things ashore. I told him I'd see him damned first. And that's all. You'll see her tomorrow. They've got three kids now—wonderful little rascals. I've a phonograph down below for him, and about a million records."

"And then you made him trader?" the mate inquired of Grief.

"What else could I do?" Grief answered. "Fuatino is a love island, and Pilsach is a lover. He knows natives, too—one of the best traders I've got, or ever had. He's responsible. You'll see him tomorrow."

"Look here, young man," Captain Glass rumbled threateningly at his mate. "Are you romantic? Because if you are, on board you stay. Fuatino's the island of romantic insanity. Everybody's in love with somebody. They live on love. It's in the milk of the coconuts, or the air, or the sea. The history of the island for the last ten thousand years is nothing but love affairs. I know. I've talked with the old men. And if I catch you starting down the beach hand in hand—"

His sudden cessation caused both the other men to look at him. They followed his gaze, which passed across them to the main rigging, and saw what he saw, a brown hand and arm, muscular and wet, being joined from overside by a second brown hand and arm. A head followed, thatched with long elfin locks, and then a face, with roguish black eyes, lined with the marks of wildwood laughter.

"My God!" Brown breathed. "It's a faun—a sea-faun."

"It's the Goat Man," said Glass.

"It is Mauriri," said Grief. "He is my own blood brother

by sacred plight of native custom. His name is mine, and mine is his."

Broad brown shoulders and a magnificent chest rose above the rail, and, with what seemed effortless ease, the whole grand body followed over the rail and noiselessly trod the deck. Brown, who might have become other things than the mate of an island schooner, was enchanted. All that he had ever gleaned from the books proclaimed indubitably the faun-likeness of this visitant of the deep. "But a sad faun," was the young man's judgment, as the golden-brown woods god strode forward to where David Grief sat up with outstretched hand.

"David," said David Grief.

"Mauriri, Big Brother," said Mauriri.

In the custom of men who have pledged blood brotherhood, each called the other, not by the other's name, but by his own. Also, they talked in the Polynesian tongue of Fuatino, and Brown could only sit and guess.

"A long swim to say *talofa*," Grief said, as the other sat and streamed water on the deck.

"Many days and nights have I watched for your coming, Big Brother," Mauriri replied. "I have sat on the Big Rock, where the blasting dynamite is kept, of which I have been made keeper. I saw you come up to the entrance and run back into darkness. I knew you waited till morning, so I followed. Great trouble has come upon us. Mataara has cried these many days for your coming. She is an old woman, and Motauri is dead, and she is sad."

"Did he marry Naumoo?" Grief asked, after he had shaken his head and sighed according to custom.

"Yes. In the end they ran to live with the goats, till

Mataara forgave, when they returned to live with her in the Big House. But he is now dead, and Naumoo soon may die. Great is our trouble, Big Brother. Tori is dead, and Tati-Tori, and Petoo, and Nari, and Pilsach, and others."

"Pilsach, too!" Grief exclaimed. "Has there been a sickness?"

"There has been much killing. Listen, Big Brother. Three weeks ago a strange schooner came. From the Big Rock I saw her topsails above the sea. She towed in with her boats, but they did not warp by the big patch, and she pounded many times. She is now on the beach, where they are strengthening the broken timbers. There are eight white men on board. They have women from some island far to the east. The women talk a language in many ways like ours, only different. But we can understand. They say they were stolen by the men on the schooner. We do not know, but they sing and dance and are happy."

"And the men?" Grief interrupted.

"They talk French. I know, for there was a mate on your schooner who talked French long ago. There are two chief men, and they do not look like the others. They have blue eyes like you, and they are devils. One is a bigger devil than the other. The other six are also devils. They do not pay us for our yams, and taro, and breadfruit. They take everything from us, and if we complain they kill us. Thus was killed Tori, and Tati-Tori, and Petoo, and others. We cannot fight, for we have no guns—only two or three old guns.

"They ill-treat our women. Thus was killed Motuaro, who made defense of Naumoo, whom they have now taken on board their schooner. It was because of this that Pilsach was killed. Him the chief of the two chief men, the Big Devil, shot once in his whaleboat, and twice when he tried to crawl up the sand of the beach. Pilsach was a brave man, and Notutu now sits in the house and cries without end. Many of the people are afraid, and have run to live with the goats. But there is not food for all in the high mountains. And the men will not go out and fish, and they work no more in the gardens because of the devils who take all they have. And we are ready to fight.

"Big Brother, we need guns, and much ammunition. I sent word before I swam out to you, and the men are waiting. The strange white men do not know you are come. Give me a boat, and the guns, and I will go back before the sun. And when you come in tomorrow we will be ready for the word from you to kill the strange white men. They must be killed. Big Brother, you have ever been of the blood with us, and the men and women have prayed to many gods for your coming. And you are come."

"I will go in the boat with you," Grief said.

"No, Big Brother," was Mauriri's reply. "You must be with the schooner. The strange white men will fear the schooner, not us. We will have the guns, and they will not know. It is only when they see your schooner come that they will be alarmed. Send the young man there with the boat."

So it was that Brown, thrilling with all the romance and adventure he had read and guessed and never lived, took his place in the sternsheets of a whaleboat, loaded with rifles and cartridges, rowed by four Raiatea sailors, steered by a golden-brown, sea-swimming faun, and directed through the warm tropic darkness toward the half-mythical love island of

Fuatino, which had been invaded by twentieth century pirates.

If a line be drawn between Jaluit, in the Marshall Group, and Bougainville, in the Solomons, and if this line be bisected two degrees south of the equator by a line drawn from Ukuor, in the Carolines, the high island of Fuatino will be raised in that sun-washed stretch of lonely sea. Inhabited by a stock kindred to the Hawaiian, the Samoan, the Tahitian, and the Maori, Fuatino becomes the apex of the wedge driven by Polynesia far to the west between Melanesia and Micronesia. And it was Fuatino that David Grief raised again next morning, two miles to the east and in direct line with the rising sun. The same whisper of a breeze held, and the *Rattler* slid through the smooth sea at a rate that would have been eminently proper for an island schooner had the breeze been thrice as strong.

Fuatino was nothing else than an ancient crater, thrust upward from the sea bottom by some primordial cataclysm. The western portion, broken and crumbled to sea level, was the entrance to the crater itself, which constituted the harbor. Thus, Fuatino was like a rugged horseshoe, the heel pointing to the west. And into the opening at the heel the *Rattler* steered. Captain Glass, binoculars in hand and peering at a homemade chart spread on top the cabin, straightened up with an expression on his face that was half alarm, half resignation.

"It's coming," he said. "Fever. It wasn't due till tomorrow. It always hits me hard, Mr. Grief. In five minutes I'll be off my head. You'll have to con the schooner in. Steward! Get my bunk ready! Plenty of blankets! Fill that hot water bottle!

It's so calm, Mr. Grief, I think you can pass the big patch without warping. Take the leading wind and shoot her. She's the only craft in the South Pacific that can do it, and I know you know the trick. You can scrape the Big Rock by just watching out for the main boom."

He had talked rapidly, almost like a drunken man, as his reeling brain battled with the rising shock of the malarial stroke. When he stumbled toward the companionway, his face was purpling and mottling as if attacked by some monstrous inflammation or decay. His eyes were setting in a glassy bulge, his hands shaking, his teeth clicking in the spasms of chill.

"Two hours to get the sweat," he chattered with a ghastly grin. "And a couple more and I'll be all right. I know the damned thing to the last minute it runs its course. Y-y-you t-t-take ch-ch-ch-ch——"

His voice faded away in a weak stutter as he collapsed down into the cabin and his employer took charge. The *Rat tler* was just entering the passage. The heels of the horseshoe island were two huge mountains of rock a thousand feet high, each almost broken off from the mainland and connected to it by a low and narrow peninsula. Between the heels was a half-mile stretch, all but blocked by a reef of coral extending across from the south heel. The passage, which Captain Glass had called a crevice, twisted into this reef, curved directly to the north heel, and ran along the base of the perpendicular Big Rock. At this point, with the main boom almost grazing the rock on the port side, Grief, peering down on the starboard side, could see bottom less than two fathoms beneath and shoaling steeply. With a whaleboat towing for steerage and as a precaution against back-drafts from the cliff, and taking advantage of a fan of breeze, he shook the *Rattler* full into it and glided by the big coral patch without warping. As it was, he just scraped, but so softly as not to start the copper.

The harbor of Fuatino opened before him. It was a circular sheet of water, five miles in diameter, rimmed with white coral beaches, from which the verdure-clad slopes rose swiftly to the frowning crater walls. The crests of the walls were saw-toothed, volcanic peaks, capped and haloed with captive trade wind clouds. Every nook and crevice of the disintegrating lava gave foothold to creeping, climbing vines and trees— a green foam of vegetation. Thin streams of water, mere films of mist, swayed and undulated downward in sheer descents of hundreds of feet. And to complete the magic of the place, the warm, moist air was heavy with the perfume of yellow-blossomed cassia.

Fanning along against light, vagrant airs, the *Rattler* worked in. Calling the whaleboat on board, Grief searched out the shore with his binoculars. There was no life. In the hot blaze of tropic sun the place slept. There was no sign of welcome. Up the beach on the north shore, where the fringe of coconut palms concealed the village, he could see the black bows of the canoes in the canoe houses. On the beach, on even keel, rested the strange schooner. Nothing moved on board her or around her. Not until the beach lay fifty yards away did Grief let go the anchor in forty fathoms. Out in the middle long years before, he had sounded three hundred fathoms without reaching bottom, which was to be expected of a healthy crater pit like Fuatino. As the chain roared and surged through the hawsehole, he noticed a number of native women in flowing *ahu's*, flower-crowned, stream out on the deck of the schooner on the beach. Also, and what they did not see, he saw from the galley the squat figure of a native steal for'ard, drop to the sand, and dive into the green screen of bush.

While the sails were furled and gasketed, awnings stretched, and sheets and tackles coiled harbor-fashion, David Grief paced the deck and looked vainly for a flutter of life elsewhere than on the strange schooner. Once, beyond any doubt, he heard the distant crack of a rifle in the direction of the Big Rock. There were no further shots.

At the end of another hour Captain Glass, under a mountain of blankets, had ceased shivering and was in the inferno of a profound sweat.

"I'll be all right in half an hour," he said weakly.

"Very well," Grief answered. "The place is dead, and I'm going ashore to see Mataara and find out the situation."

"It's a tough bunch; keep your eyes open," the captain warned him. "If you're not back in an hour, send word off."

Grief took the steering sweep, and four of his Raiatea men bent to the oars. As they landed on the beach he looked curiously at the women under the schooner's awning. He waved his hand tentatively, and they, after giggling, waved back.

"*Talofa!*" he called.

They understood the greeting, but replied, "*Iorana*," and he knew they came from the Society Group.

"Huaheine," one of his sailors unhesitatingly named their island. Grief asked them whence they came, and with giggles and laughter they replied, "Huaheine."

"It looks like old Dupuy's schooner," Grief said, in Tahitian, speaking in a low voice. "Don't look too hard. What do you think, eh? Isn't it the *Valetta*?"

As the men climbed out and lifted the whaleboat slightly up the beach they stole careless glances at the vessel.

"It is the *Valetta*," Taute said. "She carried away her topmast seven years ago. At Papeete they rigged a new one. It was ten feet shorter. That is the one."

"Go over and talk with the women. You can almost *see* Huaheine from Raiatea, and you'll be sure to know some of them. Find out all you can. And if any of the white men show up, don't start a row."

An army of hermit crabs scuttled and rustled away before him as he advanced up the beach, but under the palms no pigs rooted and grunted. The coconuts lay where they had fallen, and at the copra sheds there were no signs of curing. Industry and tidiness had vanished. Grass house after grass house he found deserted. Once he came upon an old man, blind, toothless, prodigiously wrinkled, who sat in the shade and babbled with fear when he spoke to him. It was as if the place had been struck with the plague, was Grief's thought, as he finally approached the Big House. All was desolation and disarray. There were no flower-crowned men and maidens, no babies rolling in the shade of the avocado trees. In the doorway, crouched and rocking back and forth, sat Mataara, the old queen. She wept afresh at the sight of him, divided between the tale of her woe—and regret that no follower was left to dispense to him her hospitality.

"And so they have taken Naumoo," she finished. "Motauri is dead. My people have fled and are starving with the goats. And there is no one to open for you even a drinking coconut. O Brother, your white brothers be devils."

"They are no brothers of mine, Mataara," Grief consoled.

"They are robbers and pigs, and I shall clean the island of them——"

He broke off to whirl half around, his hand flashing to his waist and back again, the big Colt leveled at the figure of a man, bent double, that rushed at him from out of the trees. He did not pull the trigger, nor did the man pause till he had flung himself headlong at Grief's feet and begun to pour forth a stream of uncouth and awful noises. Grief recognized the creature as the one he had seen steal from the *Valetta* and dive into the bush; but not until he raised him up and watched the contortions of the harelipped mouth could he understand what he uttered.

"Save me, master, save me!" the man yammered in English, though he was unmistakably a South Sea native. "I know you! Save me!"

And he broke into a wild outpour of incoherence that did not cease until Grief seized him by the shoulders and shook him into silence.

"I know you," Grief said. "You were cook in the French Hotel at Papeete two years ago. Everybody called you 'Hare-Lip.' "

The man nodded violently.

"I am now cook of the *Valetta*," he spat and spluttered, his mouth writhing in a fearful struggle with its defect. "I know you. I saw you at the hotel. I saw you at Lavina's. I saw you on the *Kittiwake*. I saw you at the *Mariposa* wharf. You are Captain Grief, and you will save me. Those men are devils. They killed Captain Dupuy. Me they made kill half the crew. Two they shot from the crosstrees. The rest they shot in the water. I knew them all. They stole the girls from Huaheine. They added to their strength with jail-men from

Noumea. They robbed the traders in the New Hebrides. They killed the trader at Vanikori, and stole two women there. They——"

But Grief no longer heard. Through the trees, from the direction of the harbor, came a rattle of rifles, and he started on the run for the beach. Pirates from Tahiti and convicts from New Caledonia! A pretty bunch of desperadoes that even now was attacking his schooner. Hare-Lip followed, still spluttering and spitting his tale of the white devils' doings.

The rifle firing ceased as abruptly as it had begun, but Grief ran on, perplexed by ominous conjectures, until, at a turn of the path, he encountered Mauriri running toward him from the beach.

"Big Brother," the Goat Man panted, "I was too late. They have taken your schooner. Come! For now they will seek for you."

He started back up the path away from the beach.

"Where is Brown?" Grief demanded.

"On the Big Rock. I will tell you afterward. Come now!"

"But my men in the whaleboat?"

Mauriri was in an agony of apprehension. "They are with the women on the strange schooner. They will not be killed. I tell you true. The devils want sailors. But you they will kill. Listen!" From the water, in a cracked tenor voice, came a French hunting song. "They are landing on the beach. They have taken your schooner—that I saw. Come!"

Careless of his own life and skin, nevertheless David Grief was possessed of no false hardihood. He knew when to fight and when to run, and that this was the time for running he had no doubt. Up the path, past the old men sitting in the shade, past Mataara crouched in the doorway of the Big

House, he followed at the heels of Mauriri. At his own heels, dog-like, plodded Hare-Lip. From behind came the cries of the hunters, but the pace Mauriri led them was heart-breaking. The broad path narrowed, swung to the right, and pitched upward. The last grass house was left behind, and through high thickets of *cassia* and swarms of great golden wasps the way rose steeply until it became a mere goat track. Pointing upward to a bare shoulder of volcanic rock, Mauriri indicated the trail across its face.

"Past that we are safe, Big Brother," he said. "The white devils never dare it, for there are rocks we roll down on their heads, and there is no other path. Always do they stop here and shoot when we cross the rock. Come!"

A quarter of an hour later they paused where the trail went naked on the face of the rock.

"Wait, and when you come, come quickly," Mauriri cautioned.

He sprang into the blaze of sunlight, and from below several rifles pumped rapidly. Bullets smacked about him, and puffs of stone dust flew out, but he got safely across. Grief followed, and so near did one bullet come that the dust of its impact stung his cheek. Nor was Hare-Lip struck, though he essayed the passage more slowly.

For the rest of the day, on the greater heights, they lay in a lava glen where terraced taro and papaya grew. And here Grief made his plans and learned about their dangerous situation.

"It was ill luck," Mauriri said. "Of all nights last night was selected by the white devils to go fishing. It was dark as we came through the passage. They were in boats and canoes. Always do they have their rifles with them. One Raiatea man they shot. Brown was very brave. We tried to get by to the top of the bay, but they headed us off, and we were driven in between the Big Rock and the village. We saved the guns and all the ammunition, but they got the boat. Thus they learned of your coming. Brown is now on this side of the Big Rock with the guns and the ammunition."

"But why didn't he go over the top of the Big Rock and give me warning as I came in from the sea?" Grief criticized.

"He knew not the way. Only the goats and I know the way. This I forgot, as I crept through the bush to gain the water and swim to you. The devils were in the bush shooting at Brown and the Raiatea men; and me they hunted till daylight, and through the morning they hunted me there in the low-lying land. Then you came in your schooner, and they watched till you went ashore, and I got away through the bush, but you were already ashore."

"You fired that shot?"

"Yes; to warn you. But they were wise and would not shoot back, and it was my last cartridge."

"Now you, Hare-Lip?" Grief said to the *Valetta's* cook.

This tale was long and painfully detailed. For a year he had been sailing out of Tahiti and through the Tuamotus on the *Valetta*. Old Dupuy was owner and captain. On his last cruise he had shipped two strangers in Tahiti as mate and supercargo. Also, another stranger he carried to be his agent on Fanriki. Raoul van Asveld and Carl Lepsius were the names of the mate and supercargo.

"They are brothers, I know, for I have heard them talk in the dark, on deck, when they thought no one listened," Hare-Lip explained.

The *Valetta* cruised through the Low Islands, picking up shell and pearls at Dupuy's stations. Frans Amundson, the third stranger, relieved Pierre Gollard at Fanriki. Pierre Gollard came on board to go back to Tahiti. The natives of Fanriki said he had a quart of pearls to turn over to Dupuy. The first night out from Fanriki there was shooting in the cabin. Then the bodies of Dupuy and Pierre Gollard were thrown overboard. The Tahitian sailors fled to the forecastle. For two days, with nothing to eat and the *Valetta* hove to, they remained below. Then Raoul van Asveld put poison in the meal he made Hare-Lip cook and carry for'ard. Half the sailors died.

"He had a rifle pointed at me, master; what could I do?" Hare-Lip whimpered. "Of the rest, two went up the rigging and were shot. Fanriki was ten miles away. The others went overboard to swim. They were shot as they swam. I, only, lived, and the two devils; for me they wanted to cook for them. That day, with the breeze, they went back to Fanriki and took on Frans Amundson, for he was one of them."

Then followed Hare-Lip's nightmare experiences as the schooner wandered on the long reaches to the westward. He was the one living witness and knew they would have killed him had he not been the cook. At Noumea five convicts had joined them. Hare-Lip was never permitted ashore at any of the islands, and Grief was the first outsider to whom he had spoken.

"And now they will kill me," Hare-Lip spluttered, "for they will know I have told you. Yet I am not all a coward, and I will stay with you, and die with you."

The Goat Man shook his head and stood up.

"Lie here and rest," he said to Grief. "It will be a long swim tonight. As for this cookman, I will take him now to the higher places where my brothers live with the goats."

"It is well that you swim as a man should, Big Brother," Mauriri whispered.

From the lava glen they had descended to the head of the bay and taken to the water. They swam softly, without splash, Mauriri in the lead. The black walls of the crater rose about them till it seemed they swam on the bottom of a great bowl. Above was the sky of faintly luminous star-dust. Ahead they could see the light which marked the *Rattler*, and from her deck, softened by distance, came a gospel hymn played on the phonograph once intended for Pilsach.

The two swimmers bore to the left, away from the captured schooner. Laughter and song followed on board after the hymn, then the phonograph started again. Grief grinned to himself at the appropriateness of it as *Lead, Kindly Light,* floated out over the dark water.

"We must take the passage and land on the Big Rock," Mauriri whispered. "The devils are holding the low land. Listen!"

Half a dozen rifle shots, at irregular intervals, attested that Brown still held the Rock and that the pirates had invested the narrow peninsula.

At the end of another hour they swam under the frowning loom of the Big Rock. Mauriri, feeling his way, led the landing in a crevice, up which for a hundred feet they climbed to a narrow ledge.

"Stay here," said Mauriri. "I go to Brown. In the morning I shall return."

"I will go with you, Brother," Grief said.

Mauriri laughed in the darkness.

"Even you, Big Brother, cannot do this thing. I am the Goat Man, and I only, of all Fuatino, can go over the Big Rock in the night. Furthermore, it will be the first time that even I have done it. Put out your hand. You feel it? That is where Pilsach's dynamite is kept. Lie close beside the wall and you may sleep without falling. I go now."

And high above the sounding surf, on a narrow shelf beside a ton of dynamite for blasting underwater coral, David Grief planned his campaign, then rested his cheek on his arm and slept.

In the morning, when Mauriri led him over the summit of the Big Rock, David Grief understood why he could not have done it in the night. Despite the accustomed nerve of a sailor for height and precarious clinging, he marveled that he was able to do it in the broad light of day. There were places, always under minute direction of Mauriri, that he leaned forward, falling, across hundred-foot deep crevices, until his outstretched hands struck a grip on the opposing wall and his legs could then be drawn across after. Once, there was a ten-foot leap, above half a thousand feet of yawning emptiness and down a fathom's length to a meager foothold. And he, despite his cool head, lost it another time on a shelf, a scant twelve inches wide, where all hand holds seemed to fail him. And Mauriri, seeing him sway, swung his own body far out and over the gulf and passed him, at the same time striking him sharply on the back to brace his reeling brain. Then it was, and forever after, that he fully knew why Mauriri had been named the Goat Man.

The defense of the Big Rock had its good points and its

defects. Impregnable to assault, two men could hold it against ten thousand. Also, it guarded the passage to the open sea. The two schooners, Raoul van Asveld, and his cutthroat following were bottled up. Grief, with the ton of dynamite which he had removed higher up the rock, was master. This he demonstrated one morning, when the schooners finally attempted to put to sea. The *Valetta* led, the whaleboat towing her manned by captured Fuatino men. Grief and the Goat Man peered straight down from a safe rock shelter, three hundred feet above. Their rifles were beside them; also a glowing fire-stick and a big bundle of dynamite sticks with fuses and detonators attached. As the whaleboat came beneath, Mauriri shook his head.

"They are our brothers. We cannot shoot."

For'ard, on the *Valetta*, were several of Grief's own Raiatea sailors. Aft stood another at the wheel. The pirates were below, or on the other schooner, with the exception of one who stood, rifle in hand, amidships. For protection he held Naumoo, the Queen's daughter, close to him.

"That is the chief devil," Mauriri whispered, "and his eyes are blue like yours. He is a terrible man. See! He holds Naumoo that we may not shoot him."

A light air and a slight tide were making into the passage, and the schooner's progress was slow.

"Do you speak English?" Grief, hidden, called down.

The man started, half lifted his rifle to the perpendicular, and looked up. There was something quick and catlike in his movements, and in his burned blond face a fighting eagerness. It was the face of a killer.

"Yes," he answered. "What do you want?"

"Turn back, or I'll blow your schooner up," Grief

warned. He blew on the fire-stick and whispered, "Tell Naumoo to break away from him and run aft."

From the *Rattler*, close astern, rifles cracked, and bullets spatted against the rock. Van Asveld laughed defiantly, and Mauriri called down in the native tongue to the woman. When directly beneath, Grief, watching, saw her jerk away from the man. At that instant Grief touched the fire-stick to the match head in the split end of the short fuse, sprang into view on the face of the rock, and dropped the dynamite. Van Asveld had managed to catch the girl and was struggling with her. The Goat Man held a rifle on him and waited a chance. The dynamite struck the deck in a compact package, bounded, and rolled into the port scupper. Van Asveld saw it and hesitated, then he and the girl ran aft for their lives. The Goat Man fired, but splintered the corner of the galley. The spattering of bullets from the *Rattler* increased, and the two on the rock crouched low for shelter and waited. Mauriri tried to see what was happening below, but Grief held him back.

"The fuse was too long," he said. "I'll know better next time."

It was half a minute before the explosion came. What happened afterward, for some little time, they could not tell, for the *Rattler's* marksmen had got the range and were maintaining a steady fire. Once, fanned by a couple of bullets, Grief risked a peep. The *Valetta*, her port deck and rail torn away, was listing and sinking as she drifted back into the harbor. Climbing on board the *Rattler* were the men and the Huaheine women who had been hidden in the *Valetta's* cabin and who had swum for it under the protecting fire. The Fuatino men who had been towing in the whaleboat had cast off the line, dashed back through the passage, and were rowing wildly for the south shore.

From the shore of the peninsula the discharges of four rifles announced that Brown and his men had worked through the jungle to the beach and were taking a hand. Grief and Mauriri joined in with their rifles. But they could do no damage, for the men of the *Rattler* were firing from the shelter of the deck house, while the wind and tide carried the schooner farther in. There was now no sign of the *Valetta*, which had sunk in the deep water of the crater.

Two things Raoul van Asveld did that showed keenness and coolness. Under the *Rattler's* rifle fire Raoul compelled the fleeing Fuatino men to come in and surrender. And at the same time, dispatching half his cutthroats in the *Rattler's* boat, he threw them ashore and across the peninsula, preventing Brown from getting away to the main part of the island. And for the rest of the morning the intermittent shooting told Grief how Brown was being driven back in again to the other side of the Big Rock. The situation was unchanged, with the exception of the loss of the *Valetta*.

The defects of the position on the Big Rock were vital. There was neither food nor water. For several nights, accompanied by one of the Raiatea men, Mauriri swam to the head of the bay for supplies. Then came the night when lights flared on the water and shots were fired. After that the water side of the Big Rock was invested as well.

"It's a funny situation," Brown remarked, who was getting all the adventure he had been led to believe resided in the South Seas. "We've got hold and can't let go, and Raoul has hold and can't let go. He can't get away, and we're liable to starve to death holding him."

"If the rain came, the rock basins would fill," said Mauriri. It was their first twenty-four hours without water. "Big Brother, tonight you and I will get water. It is work for strong men."

That night, with coconut calabashes, each of quart capacity and tightly stoppered, he led Grief down to the water from the peninsula side of the Big Rock. They swam out not more than a hundred feet. Beyond, they could hear the occasional click of an oar or the knock of a paddle against a canoe, and sometimes they saw the flare of matches as the men in the guarding boats lighted cigarettes or pipes.

"Wait here," whispered Mauriri carefully, "and hold the calabashes."

Turning over, he swam down. Grief, face downward, watched his phosphorescent track glimmer, and dim, and vanish. A long minute afterward Mauriri broke surface noiselessly at Grief's side.

"Here! Drink!"

The calabash was full, and Grief drank sweet fresh water which had come up from the depths of the salt.

"It flows out from the land," said Mauriri.

"On the bottom?"

"No. The bottom is as far below as the mountains are above. Fifty feet down it flows. Swim down until you feel its coolness."

Several times filling and emptying his lungs in diver fashion, Grief turned over and went down through the water. Salt it was to his lips, and warm to his flesh; but at last, deep down, it perceptibly chilled and tasted brackish. Then, suddenly, his body entered the cold, subterranean stream. He removed the small stopper from the calabash, and as the

sweet water gurgled into it, he saw the phosphorescent glimmer of a shark, like a sea ghost, drift sluggishly by.

Thereafter, holding the growing weight of the calabashes,
he remained on the surface, while Mauriri took them down,
one by one, and filled them.

"There are sharks," Grief said, as they swam back to shore.

"Pooh!" was the answer. "They are fish sharks. We of
Fuatino are brothers to the fish sharks."

"But the tiger sharks? I have seen them here."

"When *they* come, Big Brother, we will have no more
water to drink—unless it rains."

A week later Mauriri and a Raiatea man swam back with
empty calabashes. The tiger sharks had arrived in the harbor.
The next day they thirsted on the Big Rock.

"We must take our chance," said Grief. "Tonight I shall
go after water with Mautau. Tomorrow night, Brother, you
will go with Tehaa."

Three quarts only did Grief get, when the tiger sharks
appeared and drove them in. There were six of them on the
Rock, and a pint a day, in the sweltering heat of the mid-
tropics, is not sufficient moisture for a man's body. The
next night Mauriri and Tehaa returned with no water. And
the day following Brown learned the full meaning of thirst,
when the lips crack to bleeding, the mouth is coated with
granular slime, and the swollen tongue finds the mouth too
small for residence.

Grief swam out in the darkness with Mautau. Turn by
turn, they went down through the salt to the cool sweet
stream, drinking their fill while the calabashes were filling.
Mautau had descended with the last calabash when Grief,
peering down from the surface, saw the glimmer of sea-ghosts

and all the phosphorescent display of struggle. He swam back alone, but without relinquishing the precious burden of full calabashes.

Of food they had little. Nothing grew on the Rock, and its sides, covered with shellfish at sea level where the surf thundered in, were too precipitous for access. Here and there, where crevices permitted, a few rank shellfish and sea urchins were gleaned. Sometimes frigate birds and other sea birds were snared. Once, with a piece of frigate bird, they succeeded in hooking a shark. After that, with jealously guarded shark meat for bait, they managed on occasion to catch more sharks.

But water remained their direst need. Mauriri prayed to the Goat God for rain. Taute prayed to the Missionary God, and his two fellow islanders, backsliding, invoked the deities of their old heathen days. Grief grinned and considered. But Brown, wild-eyed with protruding blackened tongue, cursed. Especially he cursed the phonograph that in the cool twilights ground out gospel hymns from the deck of the *Rattler*. One hymn in particular, *Beyond the Smiling and the Weeping*, drove him to madness. It seemed a favorite on board the schooner, for it was played most of all. Brown, hungry and thirsty, half out of his head from weakness and suffering, could lie among the rocks with equanimity and listen to the tinkling of ukuleles and guitars, and the hulas and himines of the Huaheine women. But when the choir voices floated over the water he was beside himself. One evening a cracked tenor took up the song with the machine:

> "Beyond the smiling and the weeping,
> I shall be soon.
> Beyond the waking and the sleeping,

Beyond the sowing and the reaping,
I shall be soon,
I shall be soon."

Then it was that Brown rose up. Again and again, blindly, he emptied his rifle at the schooner. Laughter floated up from the men and women, and from the peninsula came a splattering of return bullets; but the cracked tenor sang on, and Brown continued to fire, until the hymn was played out.

It was that night that Grief and Mauriri came back with but one calabash of water. A patch of skin six inches long was missing from Grief's shoulder in token of the scrape of the sandpaper hide of a shark whose dash he had eluded.

In the early morning of another day, before the sun-blaze had gained its full strength, came an offer of a parley from Raoul van Asveld.

Brown brought the word in from the outpost among the rocks a hundred yards away. Grief was squatted over a small fire, broiling a strip of shark flesh. The last twenty-four hours had been lucky. Seaweed and sea urchins had been gathered. Tehaa had caught a shark, and Mauriri had captured a fair-sized octopus at the base of the crevice where the dynamite was stored. Then, too, in the darkness they had made two successful swims for water before the tiger sharks had nosed them out.

"Said he'd like to come in and talk with you," Brown said. "But I know what the brute is after. Wants to see how near starved to death we are."

"Bring him in," Grief said.

"And then we will kill him," the Goat Man cried joyously.
Grief shook his head.

"But he is a killer of men, Big Brother, a beast and a
devil," the Goat Man protested.

"He must not be killed, Brother. It should be our way not
to break our word."

"It is a foolish way."

"Still it should be our way," Grief answered gravely, turning the strip of shark meat over on the coals and noting the
hungry sniff and look of Tehaa. "Don't do that, Tehaa, when
the Big Devil comes. Look as if you and hunger were
strangers. Here, cook those sea urchins, and you, Big Brother,
cook the squid. We will have the Big Devil to feast with us.
Spare nothing. Cook all."

And, still broiling meat, Grief arose as Raoul van Asveld,
followed by a large Irish terrier, strode into camp. Raoul
did not make the mistake of holding out his hand.

"Hello!" he said. "I've heard of you."

"I wish I'd never heard of you," Grief answered.

"Same here," was the response. "At first, before I knew
who it was, I thought I had to deal with an ordinary trading
captain. That's why you've got me bottled up."

"And I am ashamed to say that I underrated you," Grief
smiled. "I took you for a thieving beachcomber, and not for
a really intelligent pirate and murderer. Hence, the loss of
my schooner. Honors are even, I fancy, on that score."

Raoul flushed angrily under his sunburn, but he contained
himself. His eyes roved over the supply of food and the full
water calabashes, though he concealed the incredulous surprise he felt. His was a tall, slender, well-knit figure, and
Grief, studying him, estimated his character from his face.

The eyes were keen and strong, but a bit too close together—
not pinched, however, but just a trifle too near to balance the
broad forehead, the strong chin and jaw, and the cheekbones
wide apart. Strength! His face was filled with it, and yet
Grief sensed in it the intangible something the man lacked.

"We are both strong men," Raoul said, with a bow. "We
might have been fighting for empires a hundred years ago."

It was Grief's turn to bow. "As it is, we are squalidly scrap-
ping over the enforcement of the laws of those empires."

"It all comes to dust," Raoul remarked sententiously,
sitting down. "Go ahead with your meal. Don't let me interrupt."

"Won't you join us?" was Grief's invitation.

The other looked at him with sharp steadiness, then accepted.

"I'm sticky with sweat," he said. "Can I wash?"

Grief nodded and ordered Mauriri to bring a calabash.
Raoul looked into the Goat Man's eyes, but saw nothing
save languid disinterest as the precious quart of water was
wasted on the ground.

"The dog is thirsty," Raoul said.

Grief nodded, and another calabash was presented to the
animal.

Again Raoul searched the eyes of the natives and learned
nothing.

"Sorry we have no coffee," Grief apologized. "You'll have
to drink plain water. A calabash, Tehaa. Try some of this
shark. There is squid to follow, and sea urchins and a seaweed salad. I'm sorry we haven't any frigate bird. The boys
were lazy yesterday, and didn't try to catch any."

With an appetite that would not have stopped at wire nails

dipped in lard, Grief ate perfunctorily, and tossed the scraps to the dog.

"I'm afraid I haven't got down to the primitive diet yet," he sighed, as he sat back. "The canned food on the *Rattler*, now I could make a hearty meal off that, but this junk ——" He took a half-pound strip of broiled shark and flung it to the dog. "I suppose I'll come to it if you don't surrender pretty soon."

Raoul laughed unpleasantly.

"I came to offer terms," he said pointedly.

Grief shook his head.

"There aren't any terms. I've got you where the hair is short, and I'm not going to let go."

"You think you can hold me in this hole!" Raoul cried.

"You'll never leave it alive, except in double irons." Grief surveyed his guest with an air of consideration. "I've handled your kind before. It's been pretty well cleaned out of the South Seas. But you are a how shall I say?—a sort of anachronism. You're a throwback, and we've got to get rid of you. Personally, I would advise you to go back to the schooner and blow your brains out. It is the only way to escape what you've got coming to you."

The parley, so far as Raoul was concerned, proved fruitless, and he went back into his own lines convinced that the men on the Big Rock could hold out for years, though he would have been swiftly unconvinced could he have observed Tehaa and the Raiateans, the moment his back was turned and out of sight, crawling over the rocks and sucking and crunching the scraps his dog had left uneaten.

"We hunger now, Brother," Grief said, "but it is better than to hunger for many days to come. The Big Devil, after feasting and drinking good water with us in plenty, will not stay long in Fuatino. Even tomorrow may he try to leave. Tonight you and I sleep over the top of the Rock, and Tehaa, who shoots well, will sleep with us if he can dare the Rock."

Tehaa, alone among the Raiateans, was cragsman enough to venture the perilous way, and dawn found him in a rock-barricaded nook, a hundred yards to the right of Grief and Mauriri.

The first warning was the firing of rifles from the peninsula, where Brown and his two Raiateans signalled the desperadoes' retreat and followed the besiegers through the jungle to the beach. From the eyrie on the face of the rock Grief could see nothing for another hour, until the *Rattler* appeared, making for the passage. As before, the captive Fuatino men towed with the whaleboat. Mauriri, under the direction of Grief, called down instructions to them as they passed slowly beneath. By Grief's side lay several bundles of dynamite sticks, well-lashed together and with extremely short fuses.

The deck of the *Rattler* was crowded. For'ard, rifle in hand, among the Raiatean sailors, stood a desperado whom Mauriri announced was Raoul's brother. Aft, by the helmsman, stood another. Attached to him, tied waist to waist, with slack, was Mataara, the old Queen. On the other side of the helmsman, his arm in a sling, was Captain Glass. Amidships, as before, was Raoul, and with him, lashed waist to waist, was Naumoo.

"Good morning, Mr. David Grief," Raoul called up.

"I warned you that only in double irons would you leave the island," Grief murmured down with a sad inflection.

"You can't kill all your people I have on board," was the answer.

The schooner, moving slowly, jerk by jerk, as the men pulled in the whaleboat, was almost directly beneath. The rowers, without ceasing, slacked on their oars, and were immediately threatened with the rifle of the man who stood for'ard.

"Throw, Big Brother!" Naumoo called up in the Fuatino tongue. "I am filled with sorrow and am willing to die. His knife is ready with which to cut the rope, but I shall hold him tight. Be not afraid, Big Brother. Throw, and throw straight, and good-bye."

Grief hesitated, then lowered the fire-stick which he had been blowing bright.

"Throw!" the Goat Man urged.

Still Grief hesitated.

"If they get to sea, Big Brother, Naumoo dies just the same. And there are all the others. What is her life against the many?"

"If you drop any dynamite, or fire a single shot, we'll kill all on board," Raoul cried up to them. "You can't kill these people, and I can. Shut up, you!"

This last was addressed to Naumoo, who was calling up in her native tongue and whom Raoul seized by the neck with one hand to choke to silence. In turn, she locked both arms about him and looked up beseechingly to Grief.

"Throw it, Mr. Grief, and be damned to them," Captain Glass rumbled in his deep voice. "They're bloody murderers. The cabin's full of them."

The desperado who was fastened to the old Queen swung

half about to menace Captain Glass with his rifle, when Tehaa, from his position farther along the Rock, pulled his trigger on him. The rifle dropped from the man's hand, and on his face was an expression of intense surprise as his legs crumpled under him and he sank down on deck, dragging the Queen with him.

"Port! Hard aport!" Grief cried.

Captain Glass and the Kanaka whirled the wheel over, and the bow of the *Rattler* headed in for the Rock. Amidships Raoul still struggled with Naumoo. His brother ran from for'ard to his aid, being missed by the fusillade of quick shots from Tehaa and the Goat Man. As Raoul's brother placed the muzzle of his rifle to Naumoo's side Grief touched the firestick to the match head in the split end of the fuse. Even as with both hands he tossed the big bundle of dynamite, the rifle went off, and Naumoo's fall to the deck was simultaneous with the fall of the dynamite. This time the fuse was short enough. The explosion occurred the instant the deck was reached, and that portion of the *Rattler*, along with Raoul, his brother, and Naumoo, forever disappeared.

The schooner's side was shattered, and she began to settle immediately. For'ard, every Raiatean sailor dived overboard. Captain Glass met the first man springing up the companionway from the cabin, with a kick full in the face, but was overborne and trampled on by the rush. Following the desperadoes came the Huaheine women, and as they went overboard, the *Rattler* sank on an even keel close to the base of the Rock. Her crosstrees still stuck out when she reached bottom.

Looking down, Grief could see all that occurred beneath the surface. He saw Mataara, a fathom deep, unfasten herself from the dead pirate and swim upward. As her head emerged she saw Captain Glass, who could not swim, sinking several yards away. The Queen, old woman that she was, turned over, swam down to him, and held him up as she struck out for the unsubmerged crosstrees.

Five heads, blond and brown, were mingled with the dark heads of Polynesia that dotted the surface. Grief, rifle in hand, watched for a chance to shoot. The Goat Man, after a minute, was successful, and they saw the body of one man sink sluggishly. But to the Raiatean sailors, big and brawny, was the vengeance given. Swimming swiftly, they singled out the blond heads and the brown. Those from above watched the four surviving desperadoes, clutched and locked, dragged far down beneath and drowned.

In ten minutes everything was over. The Huaheine women, laughing and giggling, were holding on to the sides of the whaleboat which had done the towing. The Raiatean sailors, waiting for orders, swam about the crosstree to which Captain Glass and Mataara clung.

"Poor old *Rattler*," Captain Glass lamented.

"Nothing of the sort," Grief called down. "In a week we'll have her raised, new timbers amidships, and we'll be on our way." And to the Queen, "How is it with you, Sister?"

"Naumoo is gone, and Motauri, Brother, but Fuatino is ours again. The day is young. Word shall be sent to all my people in the high places with the goats. And tonight, once again, and as never before, we shall feast and rejoice in the Big House."

"She's been needing new timbers abaft the beam there for years," commented Captain Glass. "But the chronometers will be out of commission for the rest of the cruise."

CHAPTER 3 · *The Jokers of New Gibbon*

I'M ALMOST afraid to let you visit New Gibbon," David Grief said. "It wasn't until you and the British gave me a free hand and let the place alone that any results were accomplished."

On the afterdeck of the *Wonder,* Wallenstein, the German Resident Commissioner from Bougainville, poured himself a long Scotch and soda and smiled.

"We take off our hats to you, Mr. Grief," he said in perfectly good English. "What you have done on this devil island is a miracle. And we shall continue not to interfere. It *is* a devil island, and old Koho is the big chief devil of them all. We never could bring him to terms. He is a liar, and he is no fool. He is a black Napoleon; a head-hunting,

70

man-eating Napoleon. How you ever pacified him is our everlasting puzzlement."

"I wouldn't call him exactly pacified," Grief answered. "Though he comes in once in a while and seems to eat out of the hand."

"That's more than we accomplished with our cruisers. Neither the Germans nor the English even laid eyes on him. You were the first."

"No; McTavish was the first," Grief disclaimed.

"Yes, I remember him—the little dried-up Scotsman." Wallenstein sipped his whiskey. "He's called the Trouble-Shooter, isn't he?"

Grief nodded.

"They say the salary you pay him is bigger than mine or the British Resident's?"

"I'm afraid it is," Grief admitted. "You see, and no offense, he's really worth it. He spends all his time wherever the trouble is. He is a wizard. He's the one who first got me onto New Gibbon. He's down on Malaita now, starting a plantation."

"The first?"

"There's not even a trading station on all Malaita. But there's our plantation now. We'll be in in half an hour." He handed the binoculars to his guest. "Those are the boat sheds to the left of the cottage. Beyond are the barracks. And to the right are the copra sheds. We dry quite a bit already. Old Koho's getting civilized enough to make his people bring in the nuts."

The *Wonder* headed directly in for the anchorage. She rose and fell lazily over a glassy swell flawed here and there by cats-paws from astern. It was the tail end of the monsoon season, and the air was heavy and sticky with tropic moisture, the sky a florid, leaden mass of formless clouds. The rugged land was swathed with cloud banks and squall wreaths, through which headlands and interior peaks thrust darkly. On one promontory, a slant of sunshine blazed torridly; on another, scarcely a mile away, a squall was bursting in a furious downpour of driving rain.

This was the dank, fat, savage island of New Gibbon, lying fifty miles to leeward of Choiseul. Geographically, it belonged to the Solomon Group. Politically, the dividing line of German and British influence cut it in half, hence the joint control by the two Resident Commissioners. In the case of New Gibbon, this control existed only on paper in the colonial offices of the two countries. There was no real control at all, and never had been. The bêche-de-mer fishermen of the old days had passed it by. The sandalwood traders, after stern experience, had given it up. The blackbirders had never succeeded in recruiting one laborer on the island, and after the schooner *Dorset* had been cut off with all hands, they left the place severely alone. Later, a German company had attempted a coconut plantation, which was abandoned after several managers and a number of contract laborers had lost their heads. German cruisers and British cruisers failed to get the natives to listen to reason. Four times the missionary societies had essayed the peaceful conquest of the island, and four times, between sickness and massacre, they had been driven away. More cruisers, more pacifications had followed —fruitlessly. The aborigines always retreated into the bush and laughed at the screaming shells. When the warships left it was an easy matter to rebuild the burned grass houses and set up the ovens in the old-fashioned way.

New Gibbon was a large island, fully one hundred and fifty miles long and half as broad. Its windward coast was ironbound, without anchorages or inlets, inhabited by scores of warring tribes—at least it had been until Koho had arisen, like a Kamehameha, and by force of arms and considerable statecraft, firmly welded the greater portion of the tribes into a confederation. His policy of permitting no intercourse with white men had been eminently right, so far as survival of his own people was concerned; and after the visit of the last cruiser he had had his own way until David Grief and McTavish the Trouble-Shooter landed on the deserted beach where once had stood the German cottage and barracks and the various English mission houses.

Followed wars, false peaces, and more wars. The wizened little Scotsman could *make* trouble as well as mend it, and not content with holding the beach, he imported bushmen from Malaita and invaded the wild pig runs of the interior jungle. He burned villages until Koho wearied of rebuilding them, and when he captured Koho's eldest son, he compelled a conference with the old chief. It was then that McTavish laid down the rate of head exchange. For each head of his own people he promised to take ten of Koho's. After Koho had learned that the Scotsman was a man of his word, the first true peace was made. In the meantime McTavish had rebuilt the cottage and barracks, cleared the jungle land along the beach, and laid out the plantation. After that he had gone on his way to mend trouble on the atoll of Tasman, where a plague of black measles had broken out and been ascribed to Grief's plantation by the devil-devil doctors. Once, a year later, he had been called back again to straighten up New Gibbon; and Koho, after paying a forced fine of two hundred thousand coconuts, decided it was cheaper to keep the peace and sell the nuts. Also, the fires of his youth had burned down. He was getting old and limped in one leg where a Lee-Enfield bullet had perforated the calf.

"I knew a chap in Hawaii," Grief said, "superintendent of a sugar plantation, who claimed he used a hammer and a tenpenny nail."

They were sitting on the broad cottage porch watching Worth, the manager of New Gibbon, doctoring the sick squad. They were New Georgia natives, a dozen of them, and the one with the aching tooth had been put back to last—Worth had failed in his first attempt. He wiped the sweat from his forehead with one hand and waved the forceps with the other.

"And broke more than one jaw," he asserted grimly.

Grief shook his head. Wallenstein smiled and elevated his brows.

"He *said* not, at any rate," Grief qualified. "He assured me, furthermore, that he always succeeded on the first trial."

"I saw it done when I was second mate on a lime-juicer," Captain Ward spoke up. "Our old man used a caulking mallet and a steel marlinespike. He took the tooth out with the first stroke, too, clean as a whistle."

"Me for the forceps," Worth muttered grimly, again inserting his pair in the native's mouth. As he pulled, the man groaned and rose in the air. "Lend a hand, somebody—hold him down," the manager appealed.

Grief and Wallenstein, on either side, gripped the native and held him. And he, in turn, struggled against them and clenched his teeth on the forceps. The group swayed back and forth. Such exertion in the stagnant heat brought the sweat out on all of them. The native sweated, too, but his was the sweat of excruciating pain. The chair on which he sat overturned. Captain Ward paused in the act of pouring himself a drink, and called encouragement. Worth pleaded with his assistants to hang on, and hung on himself, twisting the tooth till it crackled; then attempting a straightaway pull.

Nor did any of them notice the little black man who limped up the steps and stood looking on. Koho was a conservative. His fathers before him had worn no clothes, and neither did he, not even a G string. The many empty perforations in nose and lips and ears told of decorative passions long since dead. The holes on both ear lobes had been torn out, but their size was attested to by the strips of withered flesh that hung down and swept his shoulders. He cared now only for utility, and in one of the half-dozen minor holes in his right ear he carried a short clay pipe. Around his waist was buckled a cheap trade-belt, and between the imitation leather and the skin was thrust the naked blade of a long knife. Suspended from the belt was his bamboo betel nut and lime box. In his hand was a short-barreled, large-bore Snider rifle. Here and there he was marred by scars, the worst being the one left by the Lee-Enfield bullet, which had withered the calf to half the size of its mate. His shrunken mouth showed few teeth left to serve him. Face and body were shrunken and withered, but his black, beady eyes, small and close together, were very bright, restless and querulous.

He looked on, grinning. His joy in the torment of the patient was natural, for the world he lived in was a world of pain. He had endured his share of it, and inflicted far more than his share on others. When the tooth parted from its hold in the jaw and the forceps raked across the other teeth and out of the mouth with a nerve-rasping sound, old Koho's eyes fairly sparkled, and he looked with glee at the poor native, collapsed on the porch floor, groaning terribly as he held his head in both hands.

"I think he's going to faint," Grief said, bending over the victim. "Captain Ward, give him a drink, please. You'd better take one yourself, Worth; you're shaking like a leaf."

"And I think I'll take one," said Wallenstein, wiping the sweat from his face. His eye caught the shadow of Koho on the floor and followed it up to the old chief himself. "Hello! Who's this?"

"Hello, Koho!" Grief said genially, though he knew better than to offer to shake hands.

It was one of Koho's *tambos*, given him by the devil-devil doctors when he was born, that never was his flesh to come in contact with the flesh of a white man. Worth and Captain Ward of the *Wonder* greeted Koho, but Worth frowned at the sight of the Snider, for it was one of *his "tambos"* that no visiting bushman should carry a weapon on the plantation. Rifles had a nasty way of going off at the hip under such circumstances. The manager clapped his hands, and a native house boy, recruited from San Cristobal, came running. At a sign from Worth, he took the rifle from the visitor's hand and carried it inside the cottage.

"Koho," Grief said, introducing the German Resident,

"this big fella marster belong Bougainville—my word, big fella marster too much."

Koho, remembering the visits of the various German cruisers, smiled with a light of unpleasant reminiscence in his eyes.

"Don't shake hands with him, Wallenstein," Grief warned. "*Tambo,* you know." Then to Koho, "My word, you get 'm too much fat stop along you. Bime by you marry along new fella Mary, eh?"

"Too old fella me," Koho answered, with a weary shake of the head. "Me no like 'm Mary. Me no like 'm food. Close up me die along altogether." He stole a significant glance at Worth, whose head was tilted back to a long glass. "Me like 'm rum."

Grief shook his head.

"*Tambo* along black fella."

"He black fella no tambo," Koho retorted, nodding toward the groaning laborer.

"He fella sick," Grief explained.

"Me fella sick."

"You fella big liar," Grief laughed. "Rum tambo, all the time tambo. Now, Koho, we have big fella talk along this big fella marster."

And he and Wallenstein and the old chief sat down on the porch to confer about affairs of state. Koho was complimented on the peace he had kept, and he, with many protestations of his aged decrepitude, swore peace again and everlasting. Then was discussed the matter of starting a German plantation twenty miles down the coast. The land, of course, was to be bought from Koho, and the price was arranged in terms of tobacco, knives, beads, pipes, hatchets, porpoise teeth and shell money—in terms of everything except rum. While the talk went on, Koho, glancing through the window, could see Worth mixing medicines and placing bottles back in the medicine cupboard. Also, he saw the manager complete his labors by taking a drink of Scotch. Koho noted the bottle carefully. And, though he hung about for an hour after the conference was over, there was never a moment when someone or other was not in the room. When Grief and Worth sat down to a business talk, Koho gave it up.

"Me go along schooner," he announced, then turned and limped out.

"How are the mighty fallen," Grief laughed. "To think that used to be Koho, the fiercest red-handed murderer in the Solomons, who defied all his life two of the great world powers. And now he's going aboard to try and cadge Denby for a drink."

For the last time in his life Denby, supercargo of the *Wonder*, perpetrated a practical joke on a native. He was in the main cabin, checking off the list of goods being landed in the whaleboats, when Koho limped down the companionway and took a seat opposite him at the table.

"Close up me die along altogether," was the burden of the old chief's plaint. All the delights of the flesh had forsaken him. "Me no like 'm Mary. Me no like 'm food. Me too much sick fella. Me close up finish." A long, sad pause, in which his face expressed unutterable concern for his stomach, which he patted gingerly and with an assumption of pain. "Belly belong me too much sick." Another pause, which was an invitation to Denby to make suggestions. Then followed a long, weary, final sigh, and a "Me like 'm rum."

Denby laughed heartlessly. He had been cadged for drinks before by the old man, but the sternest *tambo* Grief and McTavish had laid down was the one forbidding liquor to the natives of New Gibbon.

The trouble was that Koho had acquired the taste. In his younger days he had learned the delights of drunkenness when he cut off the *Dorset*, but unfortunately he had learned it along with all his tribesmen, and the supply had not held out long. Later, when he led his naked warriors down to the destruction of the German plantation, he was wiser, and he appropriated all the liquors for his sole use. The result had been a gorgeous mixed drunk, on a dozen different sorts of drink, ranging from beer doctored with quinine to absinthe and apricot brandy. The drunk had lasted for months, and it had left him with a thirst that would remain with him until he died. This craving was to him expressed in terms of tingling sensations crawling warmly and deliciously in his brain, of good feeling, well being and high exultation. And in his barren old age when women and feasting were a weariness and old hates had smouldered down, he desired more and more the revivifying fire that came liquid out of bottles—out of all sorts of bottles—for he remembered them well. He would sit in the sun for hours, drooling in mournful contemplation of the great orgy which had been his when the German plantation was cleaned out.

Denby was sympathetic. He sought out the old chief's symptoms and offered him dyspepsia tablets from the medicine chest, pills, and a varied assortment of harmless tablets and capsules. But Koho steadfastly declined. When he cut the

Dorset off, he had bitten through a capsule of quinine; in addition, two of his warriors had partaken of a white powder and laid down and died very violently in a very short time. No; he did not believe in drugs. But the liquids from bottles, the cool-flaming youth-givers and warm-glowing dream-makers. No wonder the white men valued them so highly and refused to dispense them.

"Rum he good fella," he repeated over and over, plaintively and with the weary patience of age.

And then Denby made his mistake and played his joke. Stepping around behind Koho, he unlocked the medicine closet and took out the four-ounce bottle labeled *Essence of Mustard*. As he made believe to draw the cork and drink the contents, in the mirror on the for'ard bulkhead he glimpsed Koho, twisted half around, intently watching him. Denby smacked his lips and cleared his throat appreciatively as he replaced the bottle. Neglecting to relock the medicine closet, he returned to his chair, and, after a decent interval, went on deck. He stood beside the companionway and listened. After several moments the silence below was broken by a fearful, wheezing, propulsive, strangling cough. He smiled to himself and returned leisurely down the companionway. The bottle was back on the shelf where it belonged, and the old man sat in the same position. Denby marvelled at his iron control. Mouth and lips and tongue—all sensitive membranes, were a blaze of fire. Koho gasped and nearly coughed several times, while involuntary tears brimmed in his eyes and ran down his cheeks. An ordinary man would have strangled. But old Koho's face was grimly composed. It dawned on him that a trick had been played, and into his eyes came an expression of hatred so abysmal that it sent chills up and down Denby's spine. Koho arose proudly.

"Me go along," he said. "You sing out one fella boat stop along me."

Having seen Grief and Worth off on a tour of the plantation, Wallenstein sat down in the big living room and with gun oil and old rags proceeded to take apart and clean his automatic. On the table beside him stood the inevitable bottle of Scotch and numerous soda bottles. Another bottle, part full, chanced to stand there. It was also labeled *Scotch,* but Worth had cautioned it contained liniment which he had mixed for the horses and neglected to put away.

As Wallenstein worked, he glanced through the window and saw Koho coming up the compound path. He was limping very rapidly, but when he came along the porch and entered the room his gait was slow and dignified. He sat down and watched the gun cleaning. Though mouth and lips and tongue were afire, he gave no sign. At the end of five minutes he spoke.

"Rum he good fella. Me like 'm rum."

Wallenstein smiled and shook his head, and then it was that his perverse imp suggested what was to be *his* last joke on a native. The similarity of the two bottles was the real suggestion. He laid his pistol parts on the table and mixed himself a long drink. Standing as he did between Koho and the table, he interchanged the two bottles, drained his glass, made as if to search for something, and left the room. From outside he heard the surprised splutter and cough; but when he returned the old chief sat as before. The liniment in the bottle, however, was lower, and it still oscillated.

Koho stood up, clapped his hands, and, when the house boy answered, signed that he desired his rifle. The boy fetched the weapon, and according to custom preceded the visitor down the pathway. Not until outside the gate did the boy turn the rifle over to its owner. Wallenstein, chuckling to himself, watched the old chief limp along the beach in the direction of the river.

A few minutes later, as he put his pistol together, Wallenstein heard the distant report of a gun. For the instant he thought of Koho, then dismissed the conjecture from his mind. Worth and Grief had taken shotguns with them, and it was probably one of their shots at a pigeon. Wallenstein lounged back in his chair, chuckled, twisted his yellow mustache, and dozed. He was aroused by the excited voice of Worth, crying out:

"Ring the big fella bell! Ring plenty too much! Ring like hell!"

Wallenstein gained the porch in time to see the manager jump his horse over the low fence of the compound and dash down the beach after Grief, riding madly ahead. A loud crackling and smoke rising through the coconut trees told the story. The boathouses and the barracks were on fire. The big plantation bell was ringing wildly as the German Resident ran down the beach, and he could see whaleboats hastily putting off from the *Wonder*.

Barracks and boathouses, grass-thatched and like tinder, were wrapped in flames.

"It was my fault," Wallenstein called. "Old Koho did it. But I let him take a drink of Worth's horse liniment."

"I guess he's headed for the bush," Worth replied. "Oliver is down there by the river. Hope he didn't get *him*."

The manager galloped away through the trees. A few minutes later, as the charred wreck of the barracks crashed in, they heard him calling and followed. On the edge of the river bank they came upon him. He still sat on his horse, very white-faced, and gazed at something on the ground. It was the body of Oliver, the young assistant manager, though it was hard to realize it, for the head was gone. The native laborers, breathless from their run in from the fields, were now crowding around, and under Grief's direction they improvised a litter for the dead man.

Wallenstein was afflicted with paroxysms of sorrow and contrition. The tears were frankly in his eyes by the time he ceased lamenting and began to swear. When he tried to seize Worth's shotgun, a fleck of foam appeared on his lips.

"None of that," Grief commanded sternly. "Straighten up, Wallenstein. Don't be a fool."

"But are you going to let him escape?" the German cried wildly.

"He has escaped. The bush begins right here at the river. You can see where he waded across. He's in the wild pig runs already. It would be like the needle in the haystack, and if we followed him some of his young men would get us. Besides, the runs are all man-trapped—you know, staked pits, poisoned thorns, and the rest. McTavish and his bushmen are the only fellows who can negotiate those runs, and three of his men were lost that way the last time. Come on back to the cottage. You'll hear the conches tonight, and the war drums—and all merry hell will break loose. They won't rush us, but keep all the boys up close to the house, Mr. Worth. Come on!"

Wallenstein proved inconsolable, until Denby, coming

ashore, confessed to the dose of essence of mustard. Thereat the German Resident became even cheerful, though he twisted his yellow mustache up more fiercely and continued to curse the Solomons with oaths culled from four languages.

Next morning, visible from the masthead of the *Wonder*, the bush was alive with signal-smokes. From promontory to promontory and back, through the solid jungle, the smoke-pillars curled and puffed and talked. Remote villages on the higher peaks beyond the farthest raids McTavish had ever driven, joined in the troubled conversation. From across the river persisted a bedlam of conches; while from everywhere, drifting for miles along the quiet air, came the deep, booming reverberations of the great war drums—huge tree trunks, hollowed by fire and carved with tools of stone and shell.

"You're all right as long as you stay close," Grief told his manager. "I've got to get along now to Guvutu. They won't come out in the open and attack you. Keep the work gangs close. Stop the clearing till this blows over. They'll get any detached gangs you send out. And, whatever you do, don't be fooled into going into the bush after Koho. If you do, he'll get you. All you've got to do is wait for McTavish. I'll send him up with a bunch of his Malaita bushmen. He's the only man who can go inside. Also, until he comes, I'll leave Denby with you. You don't mind, do you, Mr. Denby? I'll send McTavish up with the *Wanda*, and you can go back on her and rejoin the *Wonder*. Captain Ward can manage without you for a trip."

"It was just what I was going to volunteer," Denby answered. "I never dreamed all this mess would be kicked up over a joke. I consider myself responsible for it."

"So am I responsible," Wallenstein broke in.

"But I started it," the supercargo urged.

"Maybe you did, but I carried it along."

"And Koho finished it," Grief said.

"At any rate, I, too, shall remain," said the German.

"I thought you were coming on to Guvutu with me," Grief protested.

"I was. But this is my jurisdiction, partly, and I have made a fool of myself in it completely. I shall remain and help set things straight again."

At Guvutu, Grief sent full instructions to McTavish by a recruiting ketch which was just starting for Malaita. Captain Ward sailed on in the *Wonder* for the Santa Cruz Islands; and Grief, borrowing a whaleboat and a crew of natives from the British Resident, crossed the channel to Guadalcanal, to examine the grass lands back of Penduffryn.

Three weeks later, with a free sheet and a lusty breeze, he threaded the coral patches and surged up the smooth water to Guvutu anchorage. The harbor was deserted, save for a small ketch which lay close in to the shore reef. Grief recognized it as the *Wanda*. She had evidently just got in by Tulagi Passage, for her native crew was still at work furling the sails. As he rounded alongside, McTavish himself extended a hand to help him over the rail.

"What's the matter?" Grief asked. "Haven't you started yet?"

McTavish nodded. "And got back. Everything's all right on board."

"How's New Gibbon?"

"All there, the last I saw of it, barrin' a few inconsequential frills that a good eye could make out lacking from the landscape."

He was a cold flame of a man, small as Koho, and as dried up, with a mahogany complexion and small, expressionless blue eyes that were more like gimlet-points. Without fear, without enthusiasm, impervious to disease and climate and sentiment, he was lean and bitter and deadly as a snake. That his present sour look boded ill news, Grief was well aware.

"Spit it out!" he said. "What's happened?"

" 'Tis a thing severely to be condemned, a damned shame, this joking with heathen aborigines," was the reply. "Also, 'tis very expensive. Come below, Mr. Grief. You'll be better for the information with a long glass in your hand. After you."

"How did you settle things?" his employer demanded as soon as they were seated in the cabin.

The little Scotsman shook his head. "There was nothing to settle. It all depends how you look at it. The other way would be to say it was settled, *entirely* settled, mind you, before I got there."

"But the plantation, man? The plantation?"

"No plantation. All the years of our work have gone for naught. 'Tis back where we started, where the missionaries started, where the Germans started—and where they finished. Not a stone stands on another at the landing pier. The houses are black ashes. Every tree is hacked down, and the wild pigs are rooting out the yams and sweet potatoes."

He paused and began fumbling in a large locker under the companion steps.

"But Worth? And Denby? And Wallenstein?"

"That's what I'm telling you. Take a look."

McTavish dragged out a sack made of rice matting and emptied its contents on the floor. David Grief pulled himself together with a jerk, for he found himself gazing fascinated at the heads of the three men he had left at New Gibbon. The yellow mustache of Wallenstein had lost its fierce curl and drooped and wilted on the upper lip.

"I don't know how it happened," the Scotsman's voice went on drearily. "But I surmise they went into the bush after the old devil."

"And where is Koho?" Grief asked.

"Back in the bush and drunk as a lord. That's how I was able to recover the heads. He was too drunk to stand. They lugged him on their backs out of the village when I rushed it. And if you'll relieve me of the heads, I'll be well obliged." He paused and sighed. "I suppose they'll have regular funerals over them and put them in the ground. But in my way of thinking they'd make excellent curios. Any respectable museum would pay five hundred apiece. Better have another drink. You're looking a bit pale—. There, put that down you, and if you'll take my advice, Mr. Grief, I would say, set your face sternly against any joking with the natives. It always makes trouble, and it is a very expensive divertissement."

CHAPTER 4 · *A Little Account with*

Swithin Hall

ITH A last long scrutiny at the unbroken circle of the sea, David Grief swung out of the cross-trees and slowly and dejectedly descended the ratlines to the deck.

"Leu-Leu Atoll is sunk, Mr. Snow," he said to the anxious-faced mate. "If there is anything to navigation, the atoll is surely under the sea, for we've sailed clear over it twice—or the spot where it ought to be. It's either that or the chronometer's gone wrong—or I've forgotten my navigation."

"It must be the chronometer," the mate reassured his owner. "I made separate sights and worked them up, and they agreed with yours."

"Yes," Grief muttered, noddingly glumly, "and where your Summer lines crossed, and mine, too, was the dead center of Leu-Leu Atoll. It must be the chronometer—slipped a cog or something."

He made a short pace to the rail and back, and cast a troubled eye at the *Uncle Toby's* wake. The schooner, with a fairly strong breeze on her quarter, was logging nine or ten knots.

"Better bring her up on the wind, Mr. Snow. Put her under easy sail and let her work to windward on two hour legs. It's thickening up, and I don't imagine we can get a star observation tonight; we'll just hold our weather position, get a latitude sight tomorrow, and run Leu-Leu down on her own latitude. That's the way all the old navigators did."

Broad of beam, heavily sparred, with high freeboard and a bluff, Dutchy bow, the *Uncle Toby* was the slowest, tubbiest, safest, and most foolproof schooner David Grief possessed. Her run was in the Banks and Santa Cruz groups and to the northwest among the several isolated atolls where his native traders collected copra, hawksbill turtle, and an occasional ton of pearl shell. Finding the skipper down with a particularly bad stroke of fever, Grief had relieved him and taken the *Uncle Toby* on her semi-annual run to the atolls. He had elected to make his first call at Leu-Leu, which lay farthest out, and now found himself lost at sea with a chronometer that played tricks.

No stars showed that night, nor was the sun visible the next day. A stuffy, sticky calm prevailed, broken by big wind squalls and heavy downpours. From fear of working too far to windward, the *Uncle Toby* was hove to, and four days and nights of cloud-hidden sky followed. Never did the sun appear, and on the several occasions that stars broke through, they were too dim and fleeting for identification. By this time even a landlubber could sense that the elements were preparing to break loose. Grief, coming on deck from consulting the barometer, which remained steadily at 29.90, encountered Jackie-Jackie, whose face was as brooding and troublous as the sky and air. Jackie-Jackie, a Tongan sailor of experience, served as a sort of bosun and semi-second mate over the mixed Kanaka crew.

"Big weather he come, I think," he said. "I see him just the same before, maybe five, six times."

Grief nodded. "Hurricane weather, all right, Jackie-Jackie. Pretty soon barometer go down—bottom fall out."

"Sure," the Tongan concurred. "He goin' to blow like hell."

Ten minutes later Snow came on deck.

"She's started," he said, "29.85, going down and pumping at the same time. It sure is hot—don't you notice it?" He brushed his forehead with his hands. "I could lose my breakfast without trying."

Jackie-Jackie grinned. "Just the same me. Everything inside walk about. Always this way before big blow. But *Uncle Toby* all right. He go through anything."

"Better rig that storm trysail on the main, and a storm jib," Grief said to the mate. "And put all the reefs into the working canvas before you furl down. No telling what we may need. Put on double gaskets while you're about it."

In another hour, the sultry oppressiveness steadily increasing and the stark calm still continuing, the barometer had fallen to 29.70. The mate lacked further patience. He ceased his restless pacing, and waved his arms.

"If she's going to come let her come!" he cried. "There's no use waiting like this! Whatever the worst is, let's have it! A fine fix—lost with a crazy chronometer and a hurricane that won't blow!"

The cloud-mussed sky turned a vague copper color, and seemed to glow like the inside of a huge heated caldron. Nobody remained below. The native sailors formed in anxious groups amidships and for'ard, talking in low voices and gazing apprehensively at the ominous sky and the equally ominous sea that breathed in long, low, oily undulations.

"Looks like petroleum mixed with castor oil," the mate grumbled, and spat his disgust overside. "My mother used to dose me with stuff like that when I was a kid. Lord, it's sure getting black!"

The lurid coppery glow had vanished, and the sky thickened and lowered until the darkness resembled a late twilight. David Grief, who knew hurricane symptoms well, nevertheless reread the *Laws of Storms*, screwing his eyes in the faint light in order to see the print. There was nothing to be done save wait for the wind, so that he might know how he lay in relation to the fast-flying and deadly center that was approaching from somewhere out of the gloom.

It was three in the afternoon with the glass sunk to 29.45 when the wind came. They could see it on the water, darkening the face of the sea, crisping tiny whitecaps as it rushed along. It was merely a stiff breeze, and the *Uncle Toby*, filling away under her storm canvas till the wind was abeam, sloshed along at a four-knot gait.

"No weight to that," Snow sneered. "And after such grand preparation!"

"Baby wind," Jackie-Jackie noted. "He grow big man pretty quick, you see."

Grief ordered the foresail put on, retaining the reefs, and the *Uncle Toby* mended her pace in the rising breeze. The wind quickly grew to man's size, but did not stop there. It merely blew hard, and harder, and kept on blowing harder, advertising each increase by lulls followed by fierce, freshening gusts. Ever it grew, until the *Uncle Toby's* rail was more often pressed under than not, while her waist boiled with foaming water which the scuppers could not carry off. Grief studied the barometer, still falling steadily.

"The center is to the south'ard," he told Snow, "and we're running across its path and into it. Now we'll turn about and run the other way. That ought to bring the glass up. Take in the foresail—it's more than she can carry already—and stand by to wear her around."

The maneuver was accomplished, and through a gloom almost like the darkness of evening, the *Uncle Toby* turned and raced madly north across the face of the storm.

"It's nip and tuck," Grief confided to the mate a couple of hours later. "The storm's swinging a big curve—there's no calculating that curve—and we may get across or the center may catch us. Thank the Lord, the glass is holding its own. It all depends on how big the curve is. The sea's too big for us to keep on. Heave her to! She'll keep working along out anyway."

"I thought I knew what wind was," Snow shouted in his owner's ear next morning. "This isn't wind. It's impossible. It must reach ninety or a hundred miles an hour in the gusts. That don't mean anything. How could I ever tell it to anybody? I couldn't. And look at that sea! I've run my Easting down, but I never saw anything like that."

Day had come, and the sun should have been up an hour, yet the best it could produce was a somber semi-twilight. The ocean was a stately procession of moving mountains. A third of a mile across yawned the valleys between the great waves. Their long slopes, shielded somewhat from the full fury of the wind, were broken by systems of smaller whitecapping waves, but from the high crests of the big waves themselves the wind tore the whitecaps as they were forming. This spume drove masthead high, and higher, horizontally, above the surface of the sea.

"We're through the worst," was Grief's judgment. "The glass is coming along all the time. The sea will get bigger as the wind eases down. I'm going to turn in. Watch for shifts in the wind. They're sure to come. Call me at eight bells."

By mid-afternoon, in a huge sea, with the wind after its last shift no more than a stiff breeze, the Tongan bosun sighted a schooner bottom up. The *Uncle Toby's* drift took them across the bow and they could not make out the name; but before night they spotted a small, round-bottom, double-ender boat, swamped but with white lettering visible on its bow. Through the binoculars, Snow made out: *Emily L. No. 3*.

"A sealing schooner," Grief said. "But what a sealer's doing in these waters is beyond me."

"Treasure hunters, maybe?" Snow speculated. "The *Sophie Sutherland* and the *Herman* were sealers, you remember, chartered out of San Francisco by fellows with maps—the kind who can always go to the right spot until they get there and don't."

After a giddy night of grand and lofty tumbling, in which, over a big and dying sea, without a breath of wind to steady her, the *Uncle Toby* rolled every person on board sick to his stomach, a light breeze sprang up and the reefs were shaken out. By midday, on a smooth ocean floor, the clouds thinned and cleared and sights of the sun were obtained. The observation gave two degrees and fifteen minutes south. But with a broken chronometer, longitude was out of the question.

"We're anywhere within five hundred and a thousand miles along that latitude line," Grief remarked, as he and the mate bent over the chart. "Leu-Leu is to the south'ard somewhere, and this section of ocean is all blank. There is neither an island nor a reef by which we can regulate the chronometer. The only thing to do——."

"Land ho, skipper!" Jackie-Jackie called down the companionway.

Grief took a quick glance at the empty blank of the chart, whistled his surprise, and sank back feebly in a chair.

"It gets me," he said. "There can't be land around here. The whole voyage has been crazy. Will you kindly go up, Mr. Snow, and see what's ailing Jackie."

"It's land all right," the mate called down a minute afterward. "You can see it from the deck—tops of coconuts—an atoll of some sort. Maybe it's Leu-Leu after all."

Grief, coming up, shook his head positively as he gazed at the fringe of palms, only the tops visible, apparently rising out of the sea.

"Haul up on the wind, Mr. Snow, close-and-by, and we'll

take a look. We can just reach past to the south, and if it
spreads off in that direction we'll hit the southwest corner."

Palms must be very near to be seen from the low deck of
a schooner, and the *Uncle Toby* quickly raised the low land
above the sea, while more palms increased the definition of
the atoll circle.

"She's a beauty," the mate remarked. "A perfect circle. . . .
Looks as if it might be eight or nine miles across. . . . Wonder
if there's an entrance to the lagoon. . . . Who knows? Maybe
it's a brand new discovery."

They coasted up the west side of the atoll, making short
tacks in to the surf-pounded coral rock and out again. From
the masthead, across the palm fringe, a Kanaka announced
the lagoon and a small island in the middle.

"I know what you're thinking," Grief said to his mate.

Snow, who had been muttering and shaking his head,
looked up with quick and challenging incredulity.

"You're thinking the entrance will be on the northwest,"
Grief went on, as if reciting. "Two cable lengths wide,
marked on the north by three separated coconuts, and on
the south by pandanus trees. Eight miles in diameter, a
perfect circle, with an island in the dead center."

"I *was* thinking that," Snow acknowledged.

"And there's the entrance opening up just where it ought
to be—."

"And the three palms," Snow almost whispered, "and the
pandanus trees. If there's a windmill on the island, it's *it*—
Swithin Hall's island. But it can't be. Everybody's been
looking for it for the last ten years."

"Hall played you a dirty trick once, didn't he?" Grief
queried.

Snow nodded. "That's why I'm working for you. He broke me flat—downright robbery. I had bought the wreck of the *Cascade*, down in Sydney, out of the first installment of a legacy from home."

"She went aground on Christmas Island, didn't she?"

"Full tilt, high and dry, in the middle of the night. They saved the passengers and the mail," Snow added. "Then I bought a little island schooner, which took the rest of my money, and I had to wait the final payment by the executors to fit her out. Meanwhile, what did Swithin Hall do—he was at Honolulu at the time—but make a straightaway run for Christmas Island. He had neither right nor title, but when I finally got there, the hull and engines were all he had left of the *Cascade*. She had a fair shipment of silk on board, too. And it wasn't even damaged. His supercargo gave it to me pretty straight, afterward. Hall cleared something like sixty thousand dollars."

Snow shrugged his shoulders and gazed bleakly at the smooth surface of the lagoon, where tiny wavelets danced in the afternoon sun.

"The wreck was mine. I bought her at public auction. I'd gambled big, and I'd lost. When I got back to Sydney, the crew and some of the tradesmen who'd extended me credit attached the schooner. I pawned my watch and sextant, shoveled coal a spell, and finally got a berth in the New Hebrides at forty dollars a month. Then I tried my luck as independent trader, went broke, took a mate's berth on a recruiter down to Tanna and over to Fiji, got a job as overseer on a German plantation back of Apia, and finally settled down on the *Uncle Toby*."

"Have you ever met Swithin Hall?"

Snow shook his head.

"Well, you're likely to meet him now. There's his windmill."

In the center of the lagoon, as they emerged from the passage, they spotted a small, densely wooded island, on which a large Dutch windmill showed plainly.

"Nobody at home from the looks of it," Grief said, "or you might have a chance to collect."

The mate's face set vindictively, and his fists clenched.

"Can't touch him legally. He's got too much money now. But I can take sixty thousand dollars' worth out of his hide. I hope he's home."

"Then I hope he is, too," Grief said, with an appreciative smile. "You got the description of his island from Bau-Oti, I suppose?"

"Yes, as pretty well everybody else has. The trouble is that Bau-Oti can't give latitude or longitude. Says they sailed a long way from the Gilberts—that's all he knows. I wonder what became of him."

"I saw him a year ago on the beach at Tahiti. Said he was thinking about shipping for a cruise through the Tuamotus. Well, here we are, getting close in. Heave the lead, Jackie-Jackie. Stand by to let go, Mr. Snow. According to Bau-Oti, anchorage three hundred yards off the west shore in nine fathoms, coral patches to the southeast. There are the patches. What do you get, Jackie?"

"Nine fathom."

"Let go, Mr. Snow."

The *Uncle Toby* swung to her chain, headsails ran down, and the Kanaka crew sprang to the fore- and main-halyards and sheets.

The whaleboat laid alongside the small, coral stone landing pier, and David Grief and his mate stepped ashore.

"You'd think the place deserted," Grief said, as they walked up a sandy path to the house. "But I smell a smell that I've often smelled. Something doing, or my nose is a liar. The lagoon is carpeted with shell and they're rotting out the meat. Get that whiff?"

Like no dwelling in the tropics was this house of Swithin Hall's. Of mission architecture, when they had entered through the unlatched screen door they found decoration and furniture of the same mission style. The floor of the big living room was covered with the finest Samoan mats. There were couches, window seats, cozy corners, and a billiard table. A sewing table and a sewing basket, spilling over with sheer linen, tokened a woman's presence. By screen and porch the blinding sunshine was subdued to a cool, dim radiance. The shine of pearl push buttons caught Grief's eye.

"Storage batteries, charged by the windmill!" he exclaimed as he pressed the buttons. "And indirect lighting!"

Hidden bulbs glowed, and the room was filled with diffused golden light. Many shelves of books lined the walls. Grief ran over their titles. A fairly well-read man himself for a sea adventurer, he glimpsed a wideness of range and breadth of taste that were beyond him. Old friends he met, and others he had heard of but never read. There were complete sets of Tolstoy, Turgenev, and Gorki; of Cooper and Mark Twain; of Hugo, Zola, and Sue; of Flaubert, De Maupassant, and Paul de Koch. He glanced curiously at the pages of Metchnikoff, Weininger, and Schopenhauer, and wonderingly at those of Ellis, Lydston, Krafft-Ebing, and Forel. Woodruff's *Expansion of Races* was in his hands when Snow returned from further exploration of the house.

"Enameled bathtub, separate shower, and a sitz bath!" he exclaimed. "Fitted up for a king! I reckon some of my money went to pay for it. The place must be occupied. I found fresh-opened butter and milk tins in the pantry, and fresh turtle meat hanging up. I'm going to see what else I can find."

Grief, too, departed, through a door that led out the opposite end of the living room. He found himself in a bedroom. Across it, he peered through a wire mesh door into a screened and darkened sleeping porch. On a couch lay a woman asleep. By her side, opened and face downward, a novel lay on a chair. From the color in her cheeks, Grief concluded that she had not been long in the tropics. After the one glimpse he stole softly back, in time to see Snow reentering the living room through the other door. By the naked arm he was clutching an age-wrinkled native who grinned in fear and made signs of dumbness.

"I found him snoozing out back," the mate said. "He's the cook, I suppose. Can't get a word out of him. What did you find?"

"A sleeping princess. S-sh! There's somebody now."

"If it's Hall," Snow muttered, clenching his fist.

Grief shook his head. "No roughhouse. There's a woman here. And if it is Hall, before we go I'll maneuver a chance for you to get action."

The door opened, and a large, heavily built man entered. In his belt was a heavy, long-barreled Colt. One quick, anxious look he gave them, then his face wreathed in a genial smile and his hand was extended.

"Welcome, strangers. But if you don't mind my asking, how, by all that's sacred, did you ever manage to find my island?"

"We were off our course," Grief answered, shaking hands.

"My name's Hall, Swithin Hall," the other said, turning to shake Snow's hand. "And I don't mind telling you you're the first visitors I've ever had."

"And this is your secret island home that's had all the beaches talking for years?" Grief answered. "Well, I know the formula now for finding it."

"How's that?" Hall asked quickly.

"Smash your chronometer, get mixed up with a hurricane, and then keep your eyes open for coconuts rising out of the sea."

"And what is your name?" Hall asked, after he had laughed perfunctorily.

"Anstey—Phil Anstey," Grief answered promptly: "Bound on the *Uncle Toby* from the Gilberts to New Guinea, and trying to find my longitude. This is my mate, Mr. Gray, a better navigator than I, but who has also lost a round to the chronometer."

Grief did not know his reason for lying, but he had felt the prompting and succumbed to it. He vaguely divined that something was wrong, but could not place his finger on it. Swithin Hall was a fat, round-faced man, with a laughing lip and laughter wrinkles in the corners of his eyes. But Grief, in his youth, had learned how deceptive this type could prove, as well as the deceptiveness of blue eyes that screened the surface with fun and hid what went on behind.

"What are you doing with my cook—lost yours and trying

to shanghai him?" Hall was saying. "You'd better let him go, if you're going to have any supper. My wife's here, and she'll be glad to meet you—dinner, she calls it, and scolds me for misnaming it, but I'm old-fashioned. My folks always ate 'dinner' in the middle of the day. Can't get over early training. Don't you want to wash up? I do. Look at me. I've been working like a dog—out with the diving crew—shell, you know. But of course you smelt it."

Snow pleaded duties on the schooner, and went on board. In addition to his repugnance at breaking bread with the man who had robbed him, it was necessary for him to impress the inviolability of Grief's lies on the Kanaka crew. By eleven o'clock Grief came on board, to find his mate waiting up for him.

"There's something doing on Swithin Hall's island," Grief said, shaking his head. "I can't make out what it is, but I get the feel of it. What does Swithin Hall look like?"

Snow shook his head.

"That man ashore there never bought the books on those shelves," Grief declared with conviction. "Nor did he ever go in for indirect lighting. He's got a surface flow of suavity, but he's rough as a rasp underneath. He's an oily bluff. And the bunch he's got with him—Watson and Gorman; they came in after you left—are real sea dogs, middle-aged, marred and battered, tough as rusty nails and twice as dangerous; real ugly customers, with guns in their belts, who don't strike me as just the right sort to be on such comradely terms with Swithin Hall. And the woman! She's a lady. She knows a whole lot of South America, and of China, too. I'm sure she's Spanish, though her English is natural. She's traveled. We talked bullfights. She's seen them in Guayaquil, in Mexico, in Seville. She knows a lot about sealskins.

"Now here's what bothers me. She knows music. I asked her if she played. And he's fixed that place up like a palace. That being so, why hasn't he a piano for her? Another thing: she's quick and lively and he watches her whenever she talks. He's on pins and needles, continually breaking in and leading the conversation. Say, did you ever hear that Swithin Hall was married?"

"I really don't know," the mate replied. "Never entered my head to ask about it."

"He introduced her as 'Mrs. Hall.' Watson and Gorman call him 'Hall.' They're a queer pair, those two men. I don't understand it at all."

"What are you going to do?" Snow asked.

"Hang around a while. There are some books ashore there I want to read. Suppose you send that topmast down in the morning and generally overhaul. We've been through a hurricane, you know. Set up the rigging while you're about it. Get things pretty well adrift—and take your time."

The next day Grief's suspicions found further nourishment. Ashore early, he strolled across the little island to the barracks occupied by the divers. They were just boarding the boats when he arrived, and it struck him that for Kanakas they behaved more like chain-gang prisoners. The three white men were there, and Grief noted that each carried a rifle. Hall greeted him jovially enough, but Gorman and Watson scowled as they grunted curt "Good Mornings."

A moment afterward one of the Kanakas, as he bent to

place his oar, favored Grief with a slow, deliberate wink. The man's face was familiar, one of the thousands of native sailors and divers he had encountered while drifting about in the island trade.

"Don't tell them who I am," Grief said, in Tahitian. "Did you ever sail for me?"

The man's head nodded and his mouth opened, but before he could speak he was suppressed by a savage "Shut up!" from Watson, who was already in the sternsheets.

"I beg pardon," Grief said.

"That's all right," Hall interposed. "The trouble is they're too much talk and not enough work. Have to be severe with them, or they wouldn't get enough shell to pay their grub."

"What was you sayin' to him?" Gorman blurted in bluntly.

"I was asking how the shell was, and how deep they were diving."

"Thick," Hall took over the answering. "We're working now in about ten fathom. It's right out there, not a hundred yards off. Want to come along?"

Half the day Grief spent with the boats, and then had lunch in the house. In the afternoon he loafed, taking a siesta in the big living room, reading, and talking for half an hour with Mrs. Hall. After dinner, he played billiards with her husband. Swithin Hall's fame at billiards was the talk of the beaches from Levuka to Honolulu. But the man Grief played with this night proved most indifferent at the game. His own wife showed herself far cleverer with the cue.

When he went on board the *Uncle Toby* Grief routed Jackie-Jackie out of bed. He described the location of the barracks, and told the Tongan to swim softly around and have a talk with the Kanakas. In two hours Jackie-Jackie was back. He shook his head as he stood dripping before Grief.

"Very funny t'ing," he reported. "One white man stop all the time. He has big rifle. He lay in water and watch. Maybe twelve o'clock, other white man come and take rifle. First white man go to bed. Other man stop now with rifle. No good. Me cannot talk with Kanakas. Me come back."

"That does it!" Grief said to Snow, after the Tongan had gone back to his bunk. "I smell something more than shell. Those three men are standing watches over their Kanakas. That man's no more Swithin Hall than I am."

Snow whistled from the impact of a new idea.

"I've got it!" he cried.

"And I'll name it," Grief retorted. "It's in your mind that the *Emily L.* was their schooner?"

"Just that. They're raising and rotting the shell *for pearls*, while she's gone for more divers, or provisions, or both."

"And I agree with you." Grief glanced at the cabin clock and started getting ready for bed. "He's a sailor. The three of them are. But they're not island men. They're new in these waters."

Again Snow whistled.

"And the *Emily L.* is lost with all hands," he said. "We know that. They're marooned here till Swithin Hall comes. Then he'll catch them with all the pearls."

"Or they'll take possession of his schooner."

"Hope they do!" Snow muttered vindictively. "Somebody ought to rob him. Wish I was in their boots. I'd balance off that sixty thousand."

A week passed, during which time the *Uncle Toby* made ready for sea, while Grief managed to allay any suspicions by

the shore crowd. Even Gorman and Watson accepted him at
his self-description. Throughout the week Grief begged and
badgered for the longitude of the island.

"You wouldn't have me leave here lost," he finally urged.
"I can't get a line on my chronometer without your longitude."

"Hall" laughingly refused.

"You're too good a navigator, Mr. Anstey, not to fetch
New Guinea or some other high land."

"And you're too good a navigator, Mr. Hall," Grief replied,
"Not to know that I can fetch your island any time by running down its latitude."

On his last evening ashore, to dinner as usual, Grief finally
got a view of the pearls he suspected they had been collecting.
"Mrs. Hall," impulsively dropping the veil of secrecy, asked
her husband to bring them out, and then had spent half
an hour showing them to Grief. His delight in them
was as genuine as his surprise that they had made so rich a
haul.

"The lagoon is virgin," "Hall" explained. "You saw yourself that most of the shell is large and old. But it's funny that
we got most of the valuable pearls in one small patch in the
course of a week. It was a little treasure house. Every oyster
in the lagoon seemed filled—seed pearls by the quart, of
course, but the perfect ones, most of that bunch there, came
out of the small patch."

Grief ran his eye over them and knew their value ranged
from one hundred to a thousand dollars each, while several
large ones went far beyond.

"Oh, the pretties! the pretties!" "Mrs. Hall" cried, bending
forward suddenly and kissing them.

A few minutes later she arose to say good night.

"It's good-bye," Grief said, as he took her hand. "We sail at daylight."

"So suddenly!" she cried, while Grief could not help seeing the quick light of satisfaction in her husband's eyes.

"Yes," Grief continued. "All the repairs are finished. I can't get the longitude of your island out of your husband, though I'm still hoping he'll relent."

"Hall" laughed and shook his head, and as his wife left the room, proposed a last farewell nightcap. They sat over it, smoking and talking.

"What do you estimate they're worth?" Grief asked, indicating the spread of pearls on the table. "I mean what the pearl buyers would give you in open market?"

"Oh, seventy-five or eighty thousand," "Hall" said carelessly.

"I'm afraid you're underestimating. I know pearls a bit. Take that biggest one. It's perfect. Not a cent less than five thousand dollars. Some millionaire will pay double that some day, when the dealers have taken their cut. And not counting the seed pearls, you've got quarts of baroques there. Baroques are coming into fashion—they're doubling in value every year."

"Hall" gave the trove of pearls a closer and longer scrutiny, estimating the different parcels and adding the sum aloud.

"You're right," he admitted. "They're worth a hundred thousand right now."

"And at what do you figure your working expenses?" Grief went on. "Your time, and your two men's, and the divers'?"

"Five thousand would cover it."

"Then they stand to net you ninety-five thousand?"

"Something like that. But why so curious?"

"Why, I was just trying——" Grief paused and drained his glass. "Just trying to reach some sort of an equitable arrangement. Suppose I should give you and your people a passage to Sydney and the five thousand dollars—or, better, seven thousand five hundred. You've worked hard."

Without commotion or muscular movement the other man became alert and tense. His round-faced geniality went out like the flame of a snuffed candle. No laughter clouded the surface of the eyes, and in their depths showed the hard dangerous soul of the man. He spoke in a low, deliberate voice.

"Now just what in hell do you mean by that?"

Grief casually relighted his cigar.

"I don't know just how to begin," he said. "The situation is—er—is embarrassing for you. You see, I'm trying to be fair. As I say, you've worked hard. I don't want to confiscate the pearls. I want to pay you for your time and trouble, and expense."

Conviction, instantaneous and absolute, froze on the other's face.

"And I thought you were vacationing in Europe," he muttered. Hope flickered for a moment. "Look here, you're joking with me. How do I know *you're* Swithin Hall?"

Grief shrugged his shoulders. "Such a joke would be in poor taste, after your hospitality. And it is in equally poor taste to have *two* Swithin Halls on the island."

"Since you're Swithin Hall, then who the devil am I? Do you know that, too?"

"No," Grief answered airily. "But I'd like to know."

"Well, it's none of your business."

"I grant it. Your identity is beside the point. Besides, I know your schooner, and I can find out from that."

"What's her name?"

"The *Emily L.*"

"Correct. I'm Captain Raffy, owner and master."

"The seal poacher? I've heard of you. What under the sun brought you down here?"

"Needed money. The seal herds are about finished."

"And these out-of-the-way places of the world are more poorly policed, eh?"

"Pretty close to it. And now about this present scrape, Mr. Hall. I can put up a nasty fight. What are you going to do about it?"

"What I said. Even better. What's the *Emily L.* worth?"

"She's seen her day. Not above ten thousand, which would be robbery. Every time she's in a rough sea I'm afraid she'll jump her ballast through the planking."

"She has jumped it, Captain Raffy. I sighted her bottom-up after the blow. Suppose we say she was worth seven thousand five hundred. I'll pay over to you fifteen thousand and give you a passage."

At that, Grief, with a sudden movement, swept the Colt from Captain Raffy's belt. "Just a necessary precaution, Captain. Now you'll go on board with me. I'll break the news to Mrs. Raffy afterward, and fetch her out to join you."

"You're behaving handsomely, Mr. Hall, I must say," Captain Raffy volunteered, as the whaleboat came alongside the Uncle Toby. "But watch out for Gorman and Watson. They're ugly customers. And, by the way, I don't like to mention it, but I've given my wife four or five pearls. Watson and Gorman were willing."

"Say no more, Captain. Say no more. They shall remain hers. Is that you, Mr. Snow? Here's a friend I want you to take charge of—Captain Raffy. I'm going ashore for his wife."

David Grief sat at Swithin Hall's library table, writing. Outside, the first pale light of dawn was showing. Grief had had a busy night. Mrs. Raffy had taken two hysterical hours to pack her and Captain Raffy's possessions. Gorman had been caught asleep, but Watson, standing guard over the divers, had shown fight. Matters did not reach the shooting stage, but only after it had been demonstrated to him that the game was up did he consent to join his companions on board. For temporary convenience, he and Gorman were shackled in the mate's room, Mrs. Raffy was confined in Grief's, and Captain Raffy was made fast to the cabin table.

Grief finished the document and read over what he had written:

From Swithin Hall, in pearls taken
from his lagoon (estimated) . $100,000.00

To Herbert Snow, paid in full for
salvage from steamship Cascade,
in pearls (estimated) $60,000.00

To Captain Raffy, salary and ex-
penses for collecting pearls . .   7,500.00

To Captain Raffy, reimbursement
for schooner Emily L., lost in
hurricane   7,500

To Mrs. Raffy, for good will, five
fair pearls (estimated) 1,100.00

To passage to Sydney, four persons,
   at $120.00 . . . .   480.00
To white lead for painting Swithin
   Hall's two whaleboats 9.00
To Swithin Hall, balance, in pearls
   (estimated) to be found in drawer
   of library table 23,411.00
   ————————————————
                          $100,000.00—$100,000.00

Grief signed and dated, paused, and added at the bottom:

P.S.—Still owing to Swithin Hall, three books, borrowed from library: Hudson's Law of Psychic Phenomena, *Zola's* Paris, *and Mahan's* Problem of Asia. *These books, or full value, can be collected of said David Grief's Sydney office.*

He switched off the electric light, picked up the bundle of books, carefully latched the front door, and went down to the waiting whaleboat.

CHAPTER 5 · *A Goboto Night*

A T GOBOTO the traders come off their schooners and the planters drift in from far, wild coasts, and one and all they assume shoes, white duck trousers, and various other appearances of civilization. At Goboto mail is received, bills are paid, and newspapers, rarely more than five weeks old, are accessible; the little island belted with coral reefs affords safe anchorage, is the steamer port of call, and serves as a distributing point for the whole wide-scattered island group.

Life at Goboto is heated, unhealthy and lurid, and for its size, asserts the distinction of more cases of acute alcoholism than any other spot in the world. Guvutu, over in the Solomons, claims that it drinks *between* drinks. Goboto does not deny this. It merely states in passing that in the Goboton chronology, no such interval as "between drinks" is known. It also points out its import statistics, which show a far larger per capita consumption of spirituous liquors. Guvutu explains this on the basis that Goboto does a larger business and has more visitors. Goboto retorts that its resident population is smaller and that its visitors are thirstier. And the discussion goes on interminably, principally because the disputants do not live long enough to settle it.

Goboto is not large. The island is only a quarter-mile in diameter, and on it are situated an Admiralty coal shed (where a few tons of coal have lain untouched for twenty years), the barracks for a handful of native laborers, a big store and warehouse with sheet-iron roofs, and a cottage inhabited by the manager and his two clerks. They are the white population. An average of one man out of the three is always to be found down with fever. The job at Goboto is a hard one. It is the policy of the company to treat its patrons well, as invading companies have found out, and it is the task of the manager and clerks to do the treating. Throughout the year traders and recruiters arrive from far, dry cruises, and planters from equally distant and dry shores, bringing with them magnificent thirsts. Goboto is the mecca of sprees, and when they have spreed, they go back to their schooners and plantations to recuperate.

Some of the less hardy require as much as six months between visits. But for the manager and his assistants there are no such intervals. They are on the spot, and week by week, blown in by monsoon or southeast trade, the schooners come to anchor, cargo'd with copra, ivory nuts, pearl shell, hawksbill turtle, and thirst.

It is a very hard job at Goboto. That is why the pay is twice that on other stations, and that is why the company selects only courageous and intrepid men for this particular station. They last no more than a year or so, when the wreckage of them is shipped back to Australia, or the remains of them are buried in the sand across on the windward side of the islet. Johnny Bassett, almost the legendary hero of Goboto, broke all records. He was a remittance man with a remarkable constitution, and he lasted seven years. His dying request was duly observed by his clerks, who pickled him in a cask of trade-rum (paid for out of their own salaries) and shipped him back to his relatives in England.

Nevertheless, at Goboto, they tried to be gentlemen. For that matter, though something was wrong with them, they *were* gentlemen, and *had been* gentlemen. That was why the great unwritten rule of Goboto was that visitors should put on pants and shoes. Breech-clouts, lava-lavas, and bare legs were not tolerated. When Captain Jensen, wildest of the blackbirders though descended from old New York blueblood stock, surged in, clad in loincloth, undershirt, two belted revolvers and a sheath knife, he was stopped at the beach. This was in the days of Johnny Bassett, ever a stickler in matters of etiquette. Captain Jensen stood up in the sternsheets of his whaleboat and denied the existence of pants on his schooner. Also, he affirmed his intention of coming ashore. They of Goboto nursed him back to health from a bullet hole through his shoulder, and in addition handsomely begged his pardon, for no pants *had* they found on his schooner. And finally, on the first day he sat up, Johnny Bassett kindly but firmly assisted his guest into a pair of pants of his own. This was the great precedent. In all the succeeding years it had never been violated. White men and pants were undivorce-able. Only aborigines ran naked. Pants constituted caste.

On this night things were, with one exception, in nowise different from any other night. Seven of them, with glimmering eyes and steady legs, had capped a day of Scotch with swizzle-sticked cocktails and sat down to dinner. Jacketed, trousered, and shod, they were: Jerry McMurtrey, the manager; Eddy Little and Jack Andrews, clerks; Captain Stapler, of the recruiting ketch *Merry*; Darby Shryleton, planter from Tito-Ito; Peter Gee, a half-caste Chinese pearl buyer who ranged from Ceylon to the Tuamotus, and Alfred Deacon, a visitor who had stopped off from the last steamer. At first, wine was served by the native servants to those that drank it, though all quickly shifted back to Scotch and soda, pickling their food as they ate it, ere it entered their calcined, pickled stomachs.

Over their coffee, they heard the rumble of an anchor chain through a hawsehole, tokening the arrival of a vessel.

"It's David Grief," Peter Gee remarked.

"How do *you* know?" Deacon demanded truculently. "You fellows seem to think a stranger will fall for anything. I've done sailing myself, and naming a craft when its sail is only a blur, or naming a man by the sound of his anchor—it's—it's unadulterated poppycock."

Peter Gee, engaged in lighting a cigarette, did not answer.

"Some of the natives can do amazing things that way," Mc-Murtrey interposed tactfully.

As with the others, this conduct of their young visitor jarred on the manager. From the moment of Peter Gee's arrival that afternoon Deacon had shown a tendency to pick on him. He had disputed his statements and been generally rude.

"Maybe it's because Peter's got Chinese blood in him," had been Andrews' hypothesis. "Deacon's South African, you know, and they're loony there about color."

"That's probably it," McMurtrey had agreed. "But we can't permit that sort of thing here, especially of a man like Peter Gee."

In this the manager had been in nowise wrong. Peter Gee was better educated than any man there, spoke better English as well as several other tongues, and knew and lived more of their own ideals of gentility than they did themselves. And, finally, he was a gentle soul. Violence he deprecated, though he had killed men in his time. Turbulence he abhorred—avoiding it like the plague.

Captain Stapler stepped in to assist McMurtrey:

"I remember, when I changed schooners and came into Altman, the natives knew it was me right off the bat. I wasn't expected, either, much less in another craft. They told the trader it was me. He used glasses, and still wouldn't believe them. But they knew. Told me afterward they could see it sticking out all over the schooner that I was running her."

Deacon ignored him, and returned to the attack on the pearl buyer.

"How do you know from the sound of his anchor that it is whatever-you-called-him?" he challenged.

"There are so many things that go to make up such a judgment," Peter Gee answered. "It's rather hard to explain. It would almost require a text book."

"I thought so," Deacon sneered. "Explanation that doesn't explain is easy."

"Who's for bridge?" Eddy Little, the second clerk, interrupted, looking up expectantly and starting to shuffle. "You'll play, won't you, Peter?"

"If he does, he's a faker," Deacon cut back. "I'm tired of all this poppycock. Mr. Gee can surprise us all by telling how he knows who that man was that just dropped anchor. After that I'll play piquet."

"I'd prefer bridge," Peter answered. "It's something like this: By the sound it was a small craft—no square-rigger. No whistle, no siren, was blown—again a small craft. It anchored close in—still again a small craft, for steamers and big ships must drop hook outside the middle shoal. Now the entrance is tortuous. There is no recruiting nor trading captain around who dares run the passage after dark. Certainly no stranger would. There are two exceptions. The first was Margonville. But he was executed by the High Court at Fiji. Remains the other exception, David Grief. Night or day, in any weather, he runs the passage. This is well known to all. A possible factor, in case Grief were somewhere else, would be some young dare-devil of a skipper. In this connection, in the first place I don't know of any, nor does anybody else. In the second place, David Grief is in these waters, cruising on the *Gunga*, which is shortly scheduled to leave here for Karo-Karo. I spoke to Grief on the *Gunga* in Sandfly Passage, day before yesterday. He was putting a trader ashore on a new station. He said he was going to call in at Babo, and then come on to Goboto. He has had ample time to get here. I have heard an anchor drop. Who else than David Grief can it be? Captain Donovan is skipper of the *Gunga*, and I know him too well to believe that he'd run in to Goboto after dark unless his owner were in charge. In a few minutes David Grief will enter through that door and say, 'In Guvutu they merely drink *between* drinks.' I'll wager two hundred and fifty dollars he's the man that enters and that his words will be, 'In Guvutu they merely drink *between* drinks.' "

Deacon was for the moment crushed. The sullen blood rose darkly in his face.

"Well, he's answered you," McMurtrey laughed genially. "And I'll back his bet myself for a couple of bucks."

"Bridge! Who's going to take a hand?" Eddy Little cried impatiently. "Come on, Peter!"

"The rest of you play," Deacon said. "He and I are going to play piquet."

"I'd prefer bridge," Peter Gee said mildly.

"Don't you play piquet?"

The pearl buyer nodded.

"Then come on. Maybe I can show I know more about that than I do about anchors."

"Now look here—" McMurtrey began.

"You can play bridge," Deacon shut him off. "We prefer piquet."

Reluctantly, Peter Gee was bullied into a game that he knew would be unpleasant.

"Only a rubber," he said, as he cut for deal.

"For how much?" Deacon asked.

Peter Gee shrugged his shoulders. "As you please."

"Hundred up—twenty-five dollars a game?"

Peter Gee agreed.

"With default double, of course—fifty dollars?"

"All right," said Peter Gee.

At another table four of the others sat at bridge. Captain Stapler, no card-player, looked on and replenished the long glasses of Scotch that stood at each man's right hand. Mc-Murtrey, with poorly concealed apprehension, followed as well as he could what went on at the piquet table. All were shocked by the behavior of the South African, and all were troubled by fear of some untoward act on his part. It was apparent that he was working up his animosity against the half-caste, and that the explosion might come any time.

"I hope Peter loses," McMurtrey said in an undertone.

"Not if he has any luck," Andrews answered. "He's a wizard at piquet. I know by experience."

That Peter Gee *was* lucky was obvious from the continual badgering by Deacon, who filled his glass frequently. He had lost the first game, and, from his remarks, was losing the second, when the door opened and David Grief entered.

"In Guvutu they merely drink *between* drinks," he remarked casually to the assembled company, and gripped the manager's hand. "Hello, Mac! My skipper's down in the whaleboat. He's got a silk shirt, a tie, and tennis shoes, all complete, but he wants you to send a pair of pants down. Mine are too small, but yours will fit him. Hello, Eddy! How's that *ngari-ngari?* You up, Jock? The miracle has happened. No one down with fever, and no one remarkably drunk." He sighed, "I suppose the night is young yet. Hello, Peter! You catch that big squall an hour after you left us? We had to let go the second anchor."

While he was being introduced to Deacon, McMurtrey dispatched a house boy with pants, and when Captain Donovan came in it was as a gentleman should—at least on Goboto.

Deacon lost the second game, and an outburst heralded the fact. Peter Gee devoted himself to lighting a cigarette and keeping quiet.

"What—quitting because you're ahead?" Deacon demanded.

Grief raised his eyebrows questioningly to McMurtrey, who frowned back his own disgust.

"I've won the rubber," Peter Gee explained.

"But I'm still entitled to win some money on a third hand. It's my deal. Come on!"

Peter Gee acquiesced, and the third game was on.

"Young punk—he needs a thrashing," McMurtrey muttered to Grief. "Come on, let's quit—I want to keep an eye on him. If he goes too far, I'll toss him out on the beach, Company instructions or no."

"Who is he?" Grief queried.

"A leftover from last steamer. Company's orders are to treat him nice; he's looking to invest in a plantation. Has a fifty thousand dollar letter of credit with him—and he's also got 'all-white South Africa' on the brain. Thinks because his skin is pure white and his father once was Attorney General in Pretoria, he can act like a louse. That's why he's picking on Peter, and you know Peter's the last man in the world to cause trouble. Damn the Company. I didn't engage to wet nurse infants with bank accounts. Come on, fill your glass, Grief. The man's contemptible."

"Maybe he's only young," Grief suggested.

"He can't hold his liquor—that's clear." The manager glared his disgust and wrath. "If he raises a hand to Peter, so help me, I'll give him a licking myself, the little overgrown punk!"

The pearl buyer pulled the pegs out of the cribbage board on which he was scoring and sat back. He had won the third game. He glanced across to Eddy Little, saying:

"I'm ready for bridge, now."

"I wouldn't be a quitter," Deacon snarled.

"Oh, really—I'm tired of the game," Peter Gee assured him with his habitual quietness.

"Come on," Deacon bullied. "One more. You can't take my money that way. I'm out seventy-five dollars. Double or nothing."

McMurtrey was about to interpose, but Grief restrained him with his eyes.

"If it positively is the last, all right," said Peter Gee, gathering up the cards. "It's my deal, I believe. As I understand it, this one is for seventy-five dollars. Either you owe me one hundred and fifty or we quit even?"

"That's it, friend. Either we break even or I pay you one hundred and fifty."

"Getting interesting, eh?" Grief remarked, drawing up a chair.

The other men stood or sat around the table, and Deacon played again in bad luck. That he was a good player was clear. The cards were merely running against him. That he could not take his ill luck with equanimity was equally clear. He was guilty of sharp, ugly curses which he snapped and growled at the imperturbable half-caste. In the end Peter Gee counted out, while Deacon had not even made his fifty points. He glowered speechlessly at his opponent.

"Looks like a default," said Grief.

"Which is double," said Peter Gee.

"No need telling me," Deacon snarled. "I've studied arithmetic. I owe you two hundred and twenty-five bucks. Take it!"

The way in which he flung the money on the table was an

insult in itself. But Peter Gee was even quieter, and flew no signals of resentment.

"You've got fool's luck, but you can't play cards—I can tell you that much," Deacon went on. "I could teach you cards."

The half-caste smiled and nodded acquiescence as he folded up the money.

"There's a little game called cassino—I wonder if you ever heard of it—a child's game?"

"I've seen it played," the half-caste murmured gently.

"Maybe you think you can play it?" snapped Deacon.

"Oh, no, not at the moment. I'm afraid I'm not up to it."

"It's a jolly game, cassino," Grief broke in pleasantly. "*I* like it very much."

Deacon ignored him.

"I'll play you fifty bucks a game—thirty-one points out," was the challenge to Peter Gee. "And I'll show you how little you know about cards. Come on! Where's a full deck?"

"No, thanks," the half-caste answered. "They need a fourth here at bridge."

"Yes," Eddy Little begged eagerly. "Come on, Peter, let's get started."

"Afraid of a little game like cassino," Deacon sneered. "Maybe the stakes are too high. I'll play you for pennies—if you say so."

The man's conduct was an affront to all of them. McMurtrey could stand it no longer.

"Now hold on, Deacon. He says he doesn't want to play. Let him alone."

Deacon turned raging upon his host; but before he could blurt out his abuse, Grief had stepped into the breach.

"*I'd* like to play cassino with you," he said.

"What do *you* know about it?"

"Not much, but I'm willing to learn."

"Well, I'm not teaching for pennies tonight."

"Oh, that's all right," Grief answered. "I'll play for almost any sum—within reason, of course."

Deacon proceeded to dispose of this intruder with one stroke.

"I'll play you five hundred dollars a game, if that won't upset you."

Grief beamed his delight. "That will be fine. Let us begin. Do you count sweeps?"

Deacon was taken aback. He had not expected a Goboton trader to be anything but crushed by such a proposition.

"Do you count sweeps?" Grief repeated. Andrews had brought him a new deck, and he was throwing away the joker.

"Certainly not," Deacon answered "That's a sissy game."

"I'm glad," Grief coincided. "I don't like sissy games either."

"You don't, eh? Well, then, I'll tell you what we'll do. We'll play for twenty-five hundred dollars a game."

Again Deacon was taken aback.

"I'm agreeable," Grief said, beginning to shuffle. " 'Cards' and 'spades' go out first, of course, and then 'big' and 'little cassino,' and the aces in the bridge order of value. Is that right?"

"You're a lot of comedians down here," Deacon laughed, but his laughter was strained. "How do I know you've got the money?"

"By the same token that I know you've got it. Mac, how's my credit with the Company?"

"All you want," the manager answered.

"You personally guarantee that?" Deacon demanded.

"I certainly do," McMurtrey said. "Depend upon it, the Company will honor his note up to and past your letter of credit."

"Low card deals," Grief said, placing the deck before Deacon on the table.

The latter hesitated in the midst of the cut and looked around with querulous misgiving at the faces of the others. The clerks and captains nodded.

"You're all strangers to me," Deacon complained. "How am I to know? Money on paper isn't always the real thing."

Then it was that Peter Gee, drawing a wallet from his pocket and borrowing a fountain pen from McMurtrey, went into action.

"I haven't started my buying yet," the half-caste explained, "so the account is intact. I'll just endorse it over to you, Grief. It's for seventy-five thousand."

Deacon intercepted the letter of credit as it was being passed across the table. He read it slowly, then glanced up at McMurtrey.

"Is this okay?"

"Yes. Just the same as your own, and just as good. The Company's paper is always good."

Deacon cut the cards, won the deal, and gave them a thorough shuffle. But luck was still against him, and he lost the game.

"Another game," he said. "We didn't say how many, and you can't quit with me a loser. I want action."

Grief shuffled and passed the cards for the cut.

"Let's play for five thousand," Deacon said, when he had

lost the second game. And when the five thousand had gone the way of the two twenty-five hundred dollar bets, he proposed to play for ten thousand.

"That's 'progression,' " McMurtrey warned, and was rewarded by a glare from Deacon. But the manager was insistent. "You don't have to play progression, Grief, unless you're foolish."

"Who's playing this game?" Deacon flamed at his host; and then, to Grief: "I've lost ten thousand to you. Will you play for ten thousand?"

Grief nodded, the fourth game began, and Deacon won. The unfairness of such betting was obvious to all of them. Though he had lost three games out of four, Deacon had lost no money. By the child's device of doubling his wager with each loss, he was bound, with the first game he won, no matter how long delayed, to be even again.

He now evinced an unspoken desire to stop, but Grief passed the deck to be cut.

"What?" Deacon cried. "You want more?"

"Haven't had anything yet," Grief murmured whimsically, as he began the deal. "Back to the usual twenty-five hundred, I suppose?"

The shame of what he had done must have even tingled in Deacon, for he answered, "No, we'll play for ten thousand. And say! Thirty-one points is too long. Why not twenty-one points out—if it isn't too rapid for you?"

"That will make it a nice, quick little game," Grief agreed.

The former method of play was repeated. Deacon lost two games, doubled the stake, and was again even. But Grief was patient, though the thing occurred several times in the next hour's play. Then happened what he was waiting for—a lengthening in the series of losing games for Deacon. The latter doubled to twenty thousand and lost, doubled to forty thousand and lost, and then proposed to double to eighty thousand.

Grief shook his head. "You can't do that, you know. You've only fifty thousand credit with the company."

"You mean you won't give me action?" Deacon asked hoarsely. "You mean that with forty thousand of my money you're going to quit?"

Grief smiled and shook his head.

"It's robbery, plain robbery," Deacon went on. "You take my money and won't give me action."

"No, you're wrong. I'm perfectly willing to give you whatever action you've got coming. You've got ten thousand dollars worth of action yet."

"Well, we'll play it," Deacon took him up. "You cut."

The game was played in silence, save for irritable remarks and curses from Deacon. Silently the onlookers filled and sipped their long Scotch glasses. Grief took no notice of his opponent's outbursts, but concentrated on the game. He was really playing cards, and there were fifty-two in the deck to keep track of, and of which he did keep track. Two-thirds of the way through the last deal he threw down his hand.

" 'Cards,' put me out," he said. "I have twenty-seven."

"If you've made a mistake," Deacon threatened, his face white and drawn.

"Then I shall have lost. Count them."

Grief passed over his stack of cards, and Deacon, with trembling fingers, verified the count. He half shoved his chair back from the table and emptied his glass. He looked about him at unsympathetic faces.

"I fancy I'll be catching the next steamer for Sydney," he said, and for the first time his speech was quiet and without bluster.

As Grief told them afterward: "Had he whined or raised a roar I wouldn't have given him that last chance. As it was, he took his medicine like a man, and I had to do it."

Deacon glanced at his watch, simulated a weary yawn, and started to rise.

"Wait," Grief said. "Do you want further action?"

The other sank down in his chair, strove to speak, but could not, licked his dry lips, and nodded his head.

"Captain Donovan here sails at daylight in the *Gunga* for Karo-Karo," Grief began with seeming irrelevance. "Karo-Karo is a ring of sand in the sea, with a few thousand coconut trees. Pandanus grows there, but they can't grow sweet potatoes nor taro. There are about eight hundred natives, a king and two prime ministers. It's a Godforsaken little hole, and once a year I send a schooner up from Goboto. The drinking water is brackish, but old Tom Butler has survived on it for a dozen years. He's the only white man there. There are no missionaries. Two native Samoan teachers were clubbed to death on the beach when they landed several years ago.

"Naturally, you are wondering what this is all about. But have patience. As I have said, Captain Donovan sails on the annual trip to Karo-Karo at daylight tomorrow. Tom Butler is old, and getting quite helpless. I've tried to retire him to Australia, but he says he wants to remain and die on Karo-

Karo, and he will in the next year or so. He's a queer old codger. Now the time is due for me to send someone else up to take the work off his hands. I wonder how you'd like the job. You'd have to stay two years.

"Hold on! I've not finished. You've talked frequently of action this evening. There's no action in betting away what you've never sweated for. The money you've lost to me was left you by your father or some other relative who did the sweating. But two years of work as trader on Karo-Karo would mean something.

"I'll bet the fifty thousand I've won from you against two years of your time. If you win, the money's yours. If you lose, you take the job at Karo-Karo and sail at daylight. Now that's what might be called real action. Will you play?"

Deacon could not speak. His throat lumped and he nodded his head as he reached for the cards.

"One thing more," Grief said. "I can do even better. If you lose, two years of your time are mine naturally without wages. Nevertheless, I'll pay you wages. If your work is satisfactory, if you observe all instructions and rules, I'll pay you twenty-five thousand dollars a year for two years. The money will be deposited with the Company, to be paid to you, with interest, when the time expires. Is that all right?"

"Too much so," Deacon stammered. "You are unfair to yourself. A trader only gets fifty or seventy-five dollars a month."

"Put it down to action, then," Grief said, with an air of dismissal. "And before we begin, I'll jot down several of the rules. These you will repeat aloud every morning during the two years—if you lose. They are for the good of your soul.

When you have repeated them aloud seven hundred and thirty Karo-Karo mornings I am confident they will be in your memory to stay. Lend me your pen, Mac. Now, let's see——"

He wrote steadily and rapidly for some minutes, then proceeded to read the matter aloud:

"I must always remember that one man is as good as another, even when he thinks he is better.

"No matter how drunk I get I must not fail to be a gentleman. A gentleman is a man who is gentle. NOTE: *It would be better not to get drunk.*

"When I play a man's game with men, I must play like a man.

"A good curse, rightly used and rarely, is an efficient thing. Too many curses spoil the cursing. NOTE: *A curse cannot change a card sequence nor cause the wind to blow.*

"There is no license for a man to be less than a man. Fifty thousand dollars cannot purchase such a license."

At the beginning of the reading, Deacon's face had gone white with anger. Then had arisen, from neck to forehead, a slow and terrible flush that deepened to the end of the reading.

"There, that will be all," Grief said, as he folded the paper and tossed it to the center of the table. "Are you still ready to play the game?"

"I deserve it," Deacon muttered brokenly. "I've been a

fool. Mr. Gee, before I know whether I win or lose, I want
to apologize. Maybe it was the whiskey, I don't know, but
I'm a damn fool."

He held out his hand, and the half-caste took it beamingly.

"Grief," Peter Gee blurted out, "the boy's all right. Call
the whole thing off and let's forget it in a final nightcap."

Grief showed signs of debating, but Deacon cried:

"No; I won't permit it. I'm not a quitter. If it's Karo-
Karo, it's Karo-Karo. That's all there is to it."

"Right," said Grief, as he began the shuffle. "If he's the
right stuff to go to Karo-Karo, Karo-Karo won't do him any
harm."

The game was close and hard. Three times they divided
the deck between them and "cards" was not scored. At the
beginning of the fifth and last deal, Deacon needed three
points to go out, and Grief needed four. "Cards" alone would
put Deacon out, and he played for "cards." He no longer
muttered or cursed, and played his best game of the evening. Incidentally he gathered in the two black aces and the
ace of hearts.

"I suppose you can name the four cards I hold," he challenged, as the last of the deal was exhausted and he picked
up his hand.

Grief nodded.

"Then name them."

"The jack of spades, the two of spades, the three of hearts,
and the ace of diamonds," Grief answered.

Those behind Deacon and looking at his hand made no
sign. Yet the naming had been correct.

"I fancy you play cassino better than I," Deacon acknowledged. "I can name only three of yours, a jack, an ace, and 'big cassino.' "

"Wrong. There aren't five aces in the deck. You've taken in three and you hold the fourth in your hand now."

"Say, you're right," Deacon admitted. "I did scoop in three. Anyway, I'll make 'cards' on you. That's all I need."

"I'll let you save 'little cassino—" Grief paused to calculate. "Yes, and the ace as well, and I'll still make 'cards' and go out with 'big cassino.' Play."

"Nobody makes 'cards,' and I win!" Deacon exulted as the last of the hand was played. "I go out on 'little cassino' and the four aces. 'Big cassino' and 'spades' only bring you to twenty."

Grief shook his head. "Some mistake, I'm afraid."

"No," Deacon declared positively. "I counted every card I took in. That's the one thing I was correct on. *I've* twenty-six, and *you've* twenty-six."

"Count again," Grief said.

Carefully and slowly, with trembling fingers, Deacon counted the cards he had taken. There were twenty-five. He reached over to the corner of the table, took up the rules Grief had written, folded them, and put them in his pocket. Then he emptied his glass, and stood up. Captain Donovan looked at his watch, yawned, and also rose.

"Going aboard, Captain?" Deacon asked.

"Yes," was the answer. "What time shall I send the whale-boat for you?"

"I'll go with you now. We'll pick up my luggage from the *Billy* as we go by. I was sailing on her for Babo in the morning."

Deacon shook hands all around, after receiving final wishes of good luck on Karo-Karo.

"Does Tom Butler play cards?" he asked Grief.

"Solitaire," was the answer.

Deacon turned toward the door, where Captain Donovan waited.

"Then I'll teach him double solitaire," he said with a sigh.

CHAPTER 6 · *The Feathers of the Sun*

I T WAS the island of Fitu-Iva—the last independent Polynesian stronghold in the South Seas. Three factors had
contributed to Fitu-Iva's independence. The first and
second were its isolation and the warlike nature of its
population. But these would not have saved it in the end had
it not been for the third—the fact that Japan, France, Great
Britain, Germany, and the United States discovered its desir-
ability simultaneously. They were like children scrambling
for a penny. They got in one another's way. The war vessels
of the five Powers cluttered Fitu-Iva's one small harbor.
There were rumors and threats of war. Over its morning toast
all the world read columns about Fitu-Iva. As an American
leatherneck epitomized it at the time, they all got their
feet in the trough at once.

132

So it was that Fitu-Iva escaped even a joint protectorate, and King Tulifau, otherwise Tui Tulifau, continued to dispense high justice and low in the frame-house palace built for him of California redwood by a Sydney trader. Not only was Tui Tulifau every inch a king, but he was every second a king. When he had ruled fifty-eight years and five months, he was only fifty-eight years and three months old. That is to say, he had ruled over five million seconds more than he had breathed, having been crowned two months before he was born.

He was a kingly King, a royal figure of a man, standing six feet and a half, and, without being excessively fat, weighing three hundred and twenty pounds. But this was not unusual for Polynesian "chief stock." Sepeli, his Queen, was six feet three inches and weighed two hundred and sixty, while her brother, Uiliami, who commanded the army in intervals of resignation from the Premiership, topped her by an inch and outweighed her by an even half-hundred weight. Tui Tulifau was a merry soul, a great feaster and drinker. So were all his people merry souls, save in anger, when, on occasion, they could be guilty even of throwing dead pigs at those who made them mad. And also on occasion they could fight like devils, as piratical sandalwood traders and blackbirders in the old days learned to their cost.

Grief's schooner, the *Cantani*, had passed the Pillar Rocks at the entrance two hours before, and crept up the harbor to the whispering flutters of a breeze that could not make up its mind to blow. It was a cool, starlit evening, and they lolled about the poop, waiting for their snail's pace to bring them to the anchorage. Willie Smee, the supercargo, emerged

from the cabin, conspicuous in his shore clothes. The mate
glanced at his shirt, of the finest and whitest silk, and giggled
significantly.

"Dance tonight, I suppose?" Grief observed.

"No," said Marsh, the mate. "It's Taitua. Willie's stuck
on her."

"Just catch me," the supercargo disclaimed.

"Then *she's* stuck on you, and it's all the same," the mate
went on. "You won't be ashore half an hour before you'll
have a flower behind your ear, a wreath on your head, and
your arm around Taitua."

"Simple jealousy," Willie Smee sniffed. "You'd like to
have her yourself, only you can't."

"I can't find shirts like that, that's why. I'll bet you half a
buck you won't sail from Fitu-Iva with that shirt."

"And if Taitua doesn't get it, it's an even bet Tui Tulifau does," Grief warned. "Better not let him spot that shirt,
or you can kiss it goodbye."

"That's right," Captain Boig agreed, turning his head
from watching the lights on the shore. "Last voyage he fined
one of my Kanakas out of a fancy belt and sheath knife." He
turned to the mate. "You can let go any time, Mr. Marsh.
Don't give too much slack. There's no sign of wind, and in
the morning we may shift opposite the copra sheds."

A minute later the anchor rumbled down. The whaleboat,
already hoisted out, lay alongside, and the shore-going party
dropped into it. Along with the Kanakas, all bent for shore,
Grief and the supercargo were in the boat. At the head of the
little coral stone pier Willie Smee, with an apologetic gurgle,
separated from his employer and disappeared down an avenue
of palms. Grief turned in the opposite direction, past the

front of the old mission church. Here, among the graves on
the beach, youths and maidens were dancing, lightly clad in
ahu's and *lava-lavas,* flower-crowned and garlanded, with great
phosphorescent hibiscus blossoms in their hair. Farther on,
Grief passed the long, grass-built *himine* house, where a few
score of the elders sat in long rows chanting the old hymns
taught them by forgotten missionaries. He passed also the
palace of Tui Tulifau, where, by the lights and sounds, he
knew the customary revelry was going on. For of the happy
South Sea isles, Fitu-Iva was the happiest. They feasted and
frolicked at births and deaths, and the dead and the unborn
were likewise feasted.

Grief held steadily along the Broom Road, which curved
and twisted through a lush growth of flowers and fernlike al-
garrobas. The warm air was rich with perfume, and overhead, outlined against the stars, were fruit-burdened mangoes, stately avocado trees, and slender-tufted palms. Every
here and there were grass houses. Voices and laughter rip-
pled through the darkness. Out on the water flickering lights
and soft-voiced choruses marked the fishers returning from
the reef.

At last Grief stepped aside from the road, stumbling over
a pig that grunted indignantly. Looking through an open
door, he saw a stout, elderly native sitting on a heap of mats
a dozen deep. From time to time, automatically, he brushed
his naked legs with a coconut-fiber flyswatter. He wore
glasses, and was reading methodically in what Grief knew to
be an English Bible. For this was Ieremia, his trader, so
named from the prophet Jeremiah.

Ieremia was lighter skinned than the Fitu-Ivans, as was
natural in a full-blooded Samoan. Educated by the mission-

aries, he had served their cause well as lay teacher over in the cannibal atolls to the westward. As a reward, he had been sent to the paradise of Fitu-Iva, where all were or had been good converts, to gather in the backsliders. Unfortunately, Ieremia had become too well-educated. A stray volume of Darwin, a nagging wife, and a pretty Fitu-Ivan widow had driven him into the ranks of the backsliders. It was not a case of apostasy. The effect of Darwin had been one of intellectual fatigue. What was the use of trying to understand this vastly complicated and enigmatical world, especially when one was married to a nagging woman? As Ieremia slackened in his labors, the mission board threatened louder and louder to send him back to the atolls, while his wife's tongue grew correspondingly sharper. Tui Tulifau was a sympathetic monarch, whose Queen, on occasions when he was particularly drunk, was known to beat him. For political reasons—the Queen belonging to as royal stock as himself and her brother commanding the army—Tui Tulifau could not divorce her, but he could and did divorce Ieremia, who promptly took up with commercial life and the lady of his choice. As an independent trader he had failed, chiefly because of the disastrous patronage of Tui Tulifau. To refuse credit to that merry monarch was to invite confiscation; to grant him credit was certain bankruptcy. After a year's idleness on the beach, Ieremia had become David Grief's trader, and for a dozen years his service had been honorable and efficient, for Grief had proven the first man who successfully refused credit to the King or who collected when it had been accorded.

Ieremia looked gravely over the rims of his glasses when his employer entered, gravely marked the place in the Bible and set it aside, and gravely shook hands.

"I am glad you came in person," he said.

"How else could I come?" Grief laughed.

But Ieremia had no sense of humor, and he ignored the remark.

"The commercial situation on this island is damn bad," he said with great solemnity. "My ledger account is shocking."

"Trade bad?"

"On the contrary. It has been excellent. The shelves are empty, exceedingly empty. But—" His eyes glistened proudly. "But there are many goods remaining in the storehouse; I have kept it carefully locked."

"Been allowing Tui Tulifau too much credit?"

"On the contrary. There has been no credit at all. And every old account has been settled up."

"I don't follow you, Ieremia," Grief confessed. "What's the joke—shelves empty, no credit, old accounts all square, storehouse carefully locked—what's the answer?"

Ieremia did not reply immediately. Reaching under the rear corner of the mats, he drew forth a large cash box. Grief noted and wondered that it was not locked. The Samoan had always been fastidiously cautious in guarding cash. The box seemed filled with paper money. He skinned off the top note and passed it over.

"There is the answer."

Grief glanced at a fairly well executed banknote. *The First Royal Bank of Fitu-Iva will pay to bearer on demand five dollars in silver,* he read. In the center was the smudged likeness of a native face. At the bottom was the signature of Tui Tulifau, and the signature of Fulualea, with the printed information appended, *Chancellor of the Exchequer.*

"Who the deuce is Fulualea?" Grief demanded. "It's Fijian, isn't it?"

"Just so. It means *feathers of the sun*. Thus does this base interloper caption himself. He has come up from Fiji to turn Fitu-Iva upside down—that is, commercially."

"One of those Levuka boys, I suppose?"

Ieremia shook his head. "No, this low fellow is a white man and a scoundrel. He has taken a noble and high-sounding Fijian name and dragged it in the dirt to suit his nefarious purposes. He has made Tui Tulifau drunk. He has made him very drunk. He has kept him very drunk all the time. In return, he has been made Chancellor of the Exchequer and other things. He has issued this false paper and compelled the people to receive it. He has levied a store tax, copra tax, and a tobacco tax. There are harbor dues and regulations, and other taxes. But the people are not taxed—only the traders. When the copra tax was levied, I lowered the price I paid for copra accordingly. The people began to grumble, and Feathers of the Sun passed a new law, putting the old price back and forbidding any man to lower it. Me he fined ten dollars and five pigs, it being well known that I possessed five pigs. You will find them entered in the ledger. Hawkins, who is trader for the Fulcrum Company, was fined first pigs, then gin, and because he continued to make loud conversation, the army came and burned his store. When I declined to sell my goods, Feathers of the Sun fined me once more and promised to burn the store if I again offended. So I sold all that was on the shelves, and there is the box full of worthless paper. I shall be chagrined if you pay me my salary in this paper, but it would be just, no more than just. Now, what is to be done?"

Grief shrugged his shoulders. "First I must see this Feathers of the Sun and size up the situation."

"Then you must see him soon," Ieremia advised. "Else he will have an accumulation of many fines against you. Thus does he absorb all the coin of the realm. He has it all now, save what has been buried in the ground."

On his way back along the Broom Road, under the lamps that marked the entrance to the palace grounds, Grief encountered a short, rotund gentleman in unstarched ducks, smooth-shaven and of florid complexion. Something about his tentative, saturated gait was familiar. Grief knew it on the instant. He had seen it before on the beaches of a dozen South Sea ports.

"Of all men, Cornelius Deasy!" he cried.

"If it ain't Grief himself, you old devil," was the return greeting, and they shook hands.

"If you'll come on board, I've some choice Irish whiskey," Grief invited.

Cornelius threw back his shoulders and stiffened.

"Nothing doin', Mr. Grief. 'Tis Fulualea I am now. No blarneyin' of old times for me. Also, and by the leave of his gracious Majesty King Tulifau, 'tis Chancellor of the Exchequer I am, an' Chief Justice I am, save in moments of royal sport when the King himself chooses to toy with the wheels of justice."

Grief whistled his amazement. "So *you're* Feathers of the Sun!"

"I prefer the native idiom," was the correction. "Fulualea, an' it please you. Not forgettin' old times, Mr. Grief, it sorrows the heart of me to break you the news. You'll have to pay your legitimate import duties same as any other trader with mind intent on robbin' the gentle Polynesian savage on coral isles implanted.—Where was I? Ah! I remember. You've violated the regulations. With malice intent have you entered the port of Fitu-Iva after sunset without sidelights burnin'. Don't interrupt. With my own eyes did I see you. For which offense you are fined the sum of twenty-five dollars. Have you any gin? 'Tis a serious offense. Not lightly are the lives of the mariners of our commodious port to be risked for the savin' of a penny'orth of oil. Did I ask: have you any gin? 'Tis the harbor master that asks."

"You've taken a lot on your shoulders," Grief grinned.

"'Tis the white man's burden. These rapscallion traders have been puttin' it all over poor Tui Tulifau, the best-hearted old monarch that ever sat a South Sea throne an' mopped grogroot from the imperial calabash. 'Tis I, Cornelius—Fulualea, rather—that am here to see justice done. Much as I dislike the doin' of it, as harbor master 'tis my duty to find you guilty of breach of quarantine."

"Quarantine?"

" 'Tis the rulin' of the port doctor. No intercourse with the shore till the ship is passed. What dire calamity to the con-fidin' native if chicken pox or whoopin' cough was aboard of you! Who is there to protect the gentle, confidin' Polynesian? I, Fulualea, Feathers of the Sun, on my high mission."

"Who in hell is the port doctor?" Grief queried.

"'Tis me, Fulualea. Your offense is serious. Consider yourself fined five cases of first-quality Holland gin."

Grief laughed heartily. "We'll compromise, Cornelius. Come aboard and have a drink."

Feathers of the Sun waved the offer aside grandly. " 'Tis bribery. I'll have none of it—me faithful to my salt. And wherefore did you not present your ship's papers? As chief of the custom house you are fined twenty-five dollars and two more cases of gin."

"Look here, Cornelius. A joke's a joke, but this one has gone far enough. This is not Levuka. I've half a mind to pull your nose for you. You can't buck me."

Feathers of the Sun retreated unsteadily and in alarm.

"Lay no violence on me," he threatened. "You're right. This is not Levuka. And by the same token, with Tui Tulifau and the royal army behind me, buck you is just the thing I can and will. You'll pay them fines promptly, or I'll confiscate your vessel. You're not the first. What does that pearl buyer, Peter Gee, do but slip into harbor, violatin' all regulations an' makin' roughhouse for the matter of a few paltry fines. No; he wouldn't pay 'em, and he's on the beach now thinkin' it over."

"You don't mean to say——"

"Sure an' I do. In the high exercise of office I seized his schooner. A fifth of the loyal army is now in charge on board of her. She'll be sold this week. Some ten tons of shell in the hold, and I'm wonderin' if I can trade it to you for gin. I can promise you a rare bargain. How much gin did you say you had?"

"Still more gin, eh?"

"An' why not? 'Tis a royal souse is Tui Tulifau. Sure it keeps my wits workin' overtime to supply him, he's that amazin' liberal with it. The whole gang of hanger-on chiefs is perpetually loaded to the gills. It's disgraceful. Are you goin' to pay them fines, Mr. Grief, or is it to harsher measures I'll be forced?"

Grief turned impatiently on his heel.

"Cornelius, you're drunk. Think it over and come to your senses. The old rollicking South Sea days are gone. You can't play tricks like that now."

"If you think you're goin' on board, Mr. Grief, I'll save you the trouble. I know your kind. I foresaw your stiff-necked stubbornness. An' it's forestalled you are. 'Tis on the beach you'll find your crew. The vessel's seized."

Grief turned back on him, still in the half-belief that he was joking. Fulualea again retreated in alarm. The form of a large man loomed beside him in the darkness.

"Is it you, Uiliami?" Fulualea crooned. "Here is another sea pirate. Stand by me with the strength of thy arm, O Herculean brother."

"Greeting, Uiliami," Grief said. "Since when has Fitu-Iva come to be run by a Levuka beachcomber? He says my schooner has been seized. Is it true?"

"It is true," Uiliami boomed from his deep chest. "Have you any more silk shirts like Willie Smee's? Tui Tulifau would like such a shirt. He has heard of it."

" 'Tis all the same," Fulualea interrupted. "Shirts or schooners, the King shall have them."

"Rather highhanded, Cornelius," Grief murmured. "It's rank piracy. You seized my vessel without giving me a chance."

"A chance is it? As we stood here, not two minutes gone, didn't you refuse to pay your fines?"

"But she was already seized."

"Sure, an' why not? Didn't I know you'd refuse? 'Tis all fair, an' no injustice done—Justice, the bright, particular star at whose shining altar Cornelius Deasy—or Fulualea, 'tis the same thing—ever worships. Get thee gone, Mr. Trader, or

I'll set the palace guards on you. Uiliami, 'tis a desperate
character, this trader man. Call the guards."

Uiliami blew the whistle suspended on his broad bare chest
by a cord of coconut fiber. Grief reached out an angry hand
for Cornelius, who stumbled into safety behind Uiliami's
massive bulk. A dozen strapping Polynesians, not one under
six feet, ran down the palace walk and ranged behind their
commander.

"Get thee gone, Mr. Trader," Cornelius ordered. "The in-
terview is terminated. We'll try your several cases in the
mornin'. Appear promptly at the palace at ten o'clock to
answer to the followin' charges, to wit: breach of the peace;
seditious and treasonable utterance; violent assault on the
chief magistrate with intent to cut, wound, maim, an' bruise;
breach of quarantine; violation of harbor regulations; and
gross breakage of custom house rules. In the mornin', fellow,
in the mornin', justice shall be done while the breadfruit
falls. And the Lord have mercy on your soul."

Before the hour set for the trial Grief, accompanied by
Peter Gee, won access to Tui Tulifau. The King, surrounded
by half a dozen chiefs, lay on mats under the shade of the
avocados in the palace compound. Early as was the hour,
palace maids were industriously serving gin. The King was
glad to see his old friend David, and regretful that he had
run foul of the new regulations. Beyond that he steadfastly
avoided discussion of the matter in hand. All protests of the
expropriated traders were washed away in proffers of gin.
"Have a drink," was his invariable reply, though once he
unbosomed himself enough to say that Feathers of the Sun
was a wonderful man. Never had palace affairs been so

prosperous. Never had there been so much money in the Treasury, nor so much gin in circulation. "Well pleased am I with Fulualea," he concluded. "Have a drink."

"We've got to get out of this pronto," Grief whispered to Peter Gee a few minutes later, "or we'll be a pair of boiled owls. Also, I am to be tried for arson, or heresy, or leprosy, or something in a few minutes, and I must collect my wits."

As they withdrew from the royal presence, Grief caught a glimpse of Sepeli, the Queen. She was peering out at her royal spouse and his fellow tipplers, and the frown on her face gave Grief his cue. Whatever was to be accomplished must be through her.

In another shady corner of the big compound Cornelius was holding court. He had been at it early, for when Grief arrived the case of Willie Smee was being settled. The entire royal army, save that portion in charge of the seized vessels, was in attendance.

"Let the defendant stand up," said Cornelius, "and receive the just and merciful sentence of the Court for licentious and disgraceful conduct unbecomin' a supercargo. The defendant says he has no money. Very well. The Court regrets it has no calaboose. In lieu thereof, and in view of the impoverished condition of the defendant, the Court fines said defendant one white silk shirt of the same kind, make and quality at present worn by defendant."

Cornelius nodded to several of the soldiers, who led the supercargo away behind an avocado tree. A minute later he emerged, minus the garment in question, and sat down beside Grief.

"What have you been up to?" Grief asked.

"Blessed if I know. What crimes have you committed?"

"Next case," said Cornelius in his most extra-legal tones. "David Grief, defendant, stand up. The Court has considered the evidence in the case, or cases, and renders the following judgment, to wit:—Shut up!" he thundered at Grief, who had attempted to interrupt. "I tell you the evidence has been considered, deeply considered. It is no wish of the Court to lay additional hardship on the defendant, and the Court takes this opportunity to warn the defendant that he is liable for contempt. For open and wanton violation of harbor rules and regulations, breach of quarantine, and disregard of shipping laws, his schooner, the *Cantani*, is hereby declared confiscated to the Government of Fitu-Iva, to be sold at public auction, ten days from date, with all appurtenances, fittings, and cargo thereunto pertaining. For the personal crimes of the defendant, consisting of violent and turbulent conduct and notorious disregard of the laws of the realm, he is fined in the sum of five hundred dollars and fifteen cases of gin. I will not ask you if you have anything to say. But will you pay? That is the question."

Grief shook his head.

"In the meantime," Cornelius went on, "consider yourself a prisoner at large. There is no calaboose in which to confine you. And finally, it has come to the knowledge of the Court, that at an early hour of this morning, the defendant did willfully and deliberately send Kanakas in his employ out on the reef to catch fish for breakfast. This is distinctly an infringement of the rights of the fisherfolk of Fitu-Iva. Home industries must be protected. This conduct of the defendant is severely reprehended by the Court, and on any repetition of the offence the offender and offenders, all and sundry, shall be immediately put to hard labor on the improvement of the Broom Road. The court is dismissed."

As they left the compound, Peter Gee nudged Grief to look where Tui Tulifau reclined on the mats. The supercargo's shirt, stretched and bulged, already encased the royal fat.

"The thing is clear," said Peter Gee, at a conference in Ieremia's house. "Deasy has gathered in about all the coin. In the meantime he keeps the King going on the gin he's captured on our vessels. As soon as he can maneuver it, he'll take the cash and skin out on your craft or mine."

"He is a low fellow," Ieremia declared, pausing in the polishing of his spectacles. "He is a scoundrel and a black-guard. He should be struck by a dead pig; by a particularly dead pig."

"*The very thing*," said Grief. "He *shall* be struck by a dead pig. Ieremia, I should not be surprised if you were the man to strike him with the dead pig. Be sure and select a par-ticularly dead one. Tui Tulifau is down at the boathouse broaching a case of my Scotch. I'm going up to the palace to work kitchen politics with the Queen. In the meantime you get a few things on your shelves from the storeroom. I'll lend you some, Hawkins. And you, Peter, tell the German store. Start in all of you, selling for paper. Remember, I'll back the losses. If I'm not mistaken, in three days we'll have a National Council or a revolution. You, Ieremia, start messengers around the island to the fishers and farmers everywhere, even to the mountain goat hunters. Tell them to assemble at the palace three days from now."

"But the soldiers," Ieremia objected.

"I'll take care of them. They haven't been paid for two months. Besides, Uiliami is the Queen's brother. Don't have too much on your shelves at a time. As soon as the soldiers show up with papers, stop selling."

"Then they will burn the stores," said Ieremia.

"Let them. King Tulifau will pay for it if they do."

"Will he pay for my shirt?" Willie Smee demanded.

"That is purely a personal and private matter between you and Tui Tulifau," Grief answered.

"It's beginning to split up the back," the supercargo lamented. "I noticed that much this morning, when he hadn't had it on ten minutes. It cost me seven bucks and I only wore it once."

"Where shall I get a dead pig?" Ieremia asked.

"Kill one, of course," said Grief. "Kill a small one."

"A small one is worth two and a half dollars."

"Then enter it in your ledger under operating expenses." Grief paused a moment. "If you want it particularly dead, it would be well to kill it at once."

"You have spoken well, David," said Queen Sepeli. "This Fulualea has brought a madness with him, and Tui Tulifau is drowned in gin. If he does not grant the big Council, I shall give him a beating. He is easy to beat when he is in drink."

She doubled up her fist, and such were her Amazonian proportions and the determination in her face that Grief knew the Council would be called. So akin was the Fitu-Ivan tongue to the Samoan that he spoke it like a native.

"And you, Uiliami," he said, "have pointed out that the

soldiers have demanded coin and refused the paper Fulualea
has offered them. Tell them to take the paper—and see that
they be paid tomorrow."

"Why trouble?" Uiliami objected. "The King remains
happily drunk. There is much money in the Treasury.
And I am content. In my house are two cases of gin and much
goods from Hawkins's store."

"Excellent pig, O my brother!" Sepeli erupted. "Has not
David spoken? Have you no ears? When the gin and the
goods in your house are gone, and no more traders come with
gin and goods, and Feathers of the Sun has run away to
Levuka with all the cash money of Fitu-Iva, what then will
you do? Cash money is silver and gold, but paper is only
paper. I tell you the people are grumbling. There is no fish
in the palace. Yams and sweet potatoes seem to have fled from
the soil, for they come not. The mountain dwellers have
sent no wild goat in a week. Though Feathers of the Sun
compels the traders to buy copra at the old price, the people
sell not, for they will have none of the paper money. Only
today have I sent messengers to twenty houses. There are no
eggs. Has Feathers of the Sun put a blight upon the hens?
I do not know. All I know is that there are no eggs. Well it
is that those who drink much eat little, else would there be
a palace famine. Tell your soldiers to receive their pay. Let it
be in his paper money."

"And remember," Grief warned, "though there be selling
in the stores, when the soldiers come with their paper it will
be refused. And in three days will be the Council, and
Feathers of the Sun will be as dead as a dead pig."

The day of the Council found the population of the island

crowded into the capital. By canoe and whaleboat, on foot and donkey back, the five thousand inhabitants of Fitu-Iva had trooped in. The three intervening days had had their share of excitement. At first there had been much selling from the sparse shelves of the traders. But when the soldiers appeared, their patronage was declined and they were told to go to Fulualea for coin. "Says it not so on the face of the paper," the traders demanded, "that for the asking the coin will be given in exchange?"

Only the strong authority of Uiliami had prevented the burning of the traders' houses. As it was, one of Grief's copra sheds went up in smoke and was duly charged by Ieremia to the King's account. Ieremia himself had been abused and mocked, and his spectacles broken. The skin was off Willie Smee's knuckles. This had been caused by three boisterous soldiers who violently struck their jaws thereon in quick succession. Captain Boig was similarly injured. Peter Gee had come off undamaged, because it chanced that it was breadbaskets and not jaws that struck him on the fists.

Tui Tulifau, with Sepeli at his side and surrounded by his convivial chiefs, sat at the head of the Council in the big compound. His right eye and jaw were swollen as if he too had engaged in assaulting somebody's fist. It was palace gossip that morning that Sepeli had administered a conjugal beating. At any rate, her spouse was sober, and his fat bulged spiritlessly through the rips in Willie Smee's silk shirt. His thirst was prodigious, and he was continually served with young drinking nuts. Outside the compound, held back by the army, was the mass of the common people. Only the lesser chiefs, village maids, village beaux, and talking men with their staffs of office were permitted inside. Cornelius Deasy, as

befitted a high and favored official, sat near to the right hand
of the King. On the left of the Queen, opposite Cornelius and
surrounded by the white traders he was to represent, sat
Ieremia. Bereft of his spectacles, he peered shortsightedly
across at the Chancellor of the Exchequer.

In turn, the talking man of the windward coast, the talking
man of the leeward coast, and the talking man of the
mountain villages, each backed by his group of lesser talking
men and chiefs, arose and made oration. What they said was
much the same. They grumbled about the paper money.
Affairs were not prosperous. No more copra was being smoked.
The people were suspicious. To such a pass had things come
that all people wanted to pay their debts and no one wanted
to be paid. Creditors made a practice of running away from
debtors. Money was cheap. Prices were going up and com-
modities were getting scarce. It cost three times the ordinary
price to buy a fowl, and then it was tough and likely to die of
old age if not immediately killed. The outlook was gloomy.
There were signs and omens. There was a plague of rats in
some districts. The crops were bad. The custard apples were
small. The best bearing avocado on the windward coast had
mysteriously shed all its leaves. The taste had gone from the
mangoes. The plantains were eaten by a worm. The fish had
forsaken the ocean and vast numbers of tiger sharks had
appeared. The wild goats had fled to inaccessible summits.
The *poi* in the *poi*-pits had turned bitter. There were rum-
blings in the mountains, nightwalking of spirits; a woman of
Punta-Puna had been struck speechless, and a five-legged she
goat had been born in the village of Eiho. And that all was
due to the strange money of Fulualea was the firm conviction
of the elders in the village councils assembled.

Uiliami spoke for the army. His men were discontented and mutinous. Though by royal decree the traders were bidden accept the money, yet did they refuse it. He would not say, but it looked as if the strange money of Fulualea had something to do with it.

Ieremia, as talking man of the traders, next spoke. When he arose, it was noticed that he stood with legs spraddled over a large grass basket. He dwelt upon the cloth of the traders, its variety and beauty and durability, which so exceeded Fitu-Ivan wet-pounded tapa, fragile and coarse. No one wore tapa any more. Yet all had worn tapa, and nothing but tapa, before the traders came. There was the mosquito netting, sold for a song, that the cleverest Fitu-Ivan net weaver could not duplicate in a thousand years. He enlarged on the incomparable virtues of rifles, axes, and steel fish-hooks, down through needles, thread and fish lines to white flour and kerosene.

He expounded at length, with firstlies and secondlies and all minor subdivisions of argument, on organization, order, and civilization. He contended that the trader was the bearer of civilization, and that the trader must be protected in his trade, else he would not come. Over to the westward were islands which would not protect the traders. What was the result? The traders would not come, and the people were like wild animals. They wore no clothes, no silk shirts (here he peered and blinked significantly at the King), and they ate one another.

The queer paper of Feathers of the Sun was not money. The traders knew what money was—they would not receive it. If Fitu-Iva persisted in trying to make them receive it, they would go away and never come back. And then the

Fitu-Ivans, who had forgotten how to make tapa, would run around naked and eat one another.

Much more he said, talking a solid hour, and always coming back to what their dire condition would be when the traders came no more. "And in that day," he concluded, "how will the Fitu-Ivan be known in the great world? *'Kai-kanak'* will men call him. 'Man-eater! *Kai-kanak!'* "

Tui Tulifau spoke briefly. The case had been presented, he said, for the people, the army, and the traders. It was now time for Feathers of the Sun to present his side. It could not be denied that he had wrought wonders with his financial system. "Many times has he explained to me the working of his system," Tui Tulifau concluded. "It is very simple. And now he will explain it to you."

It was a conspiracy of the white traders, Cornelius contended. Ieremia was right so far as the manifold blessings of white flour and kerosene were concerned. Fitu-Iva did not want to become *kai-kanak*. Fitu-Iva wanted civilization; it wanted more and more civilization. Now that was the very point, and they must follow him closely. Paper money was an earmark of higher civilization. That was why he, Feathers of the Sun, had introduced it. And that was why the traders opposed it. They did not want to see Fitu-Iva civilized. Why did they come across the far ocean stretches with their goods to Fitu-Iva? He, Feathers of the Sun, would tell the traders why, to their faces, in grand Council assembled. In their own countries men were too civilized to let the traders make the immense profits that they made out of the Fitu-Ivans. If the Fitu-Ivans became properly civilized, the trade of the traders would be gone. In that day every Fitu-Ivan could become a trader if he pleased.

That was why the white traders fought the system of paper money that he, Feathers of the Sun, had brought. Why was he called Feathers of the Sun? Because he was the Light-Bringer from the World Beyond the Sky. The paper money was the light. The robbing white traders could not flourish in the light. Therefore they fought the light.

He would prove it to the good people of Fitu-Iva, and he would prove it out of the mouths of his enemies. It was a well-known fact that all highly civilized countries had paper money systems. He would ask Ieremia if this was not so.

Ieremia did not answer.

"You see," Cornelius went on, "he makes no answer. He cannot deny what is true. England, France, Germany, America, all the great *Papalangi* countries, have the paper-money system. It works. From century to century it works. I challenge you, Ieremia, as an honest man, as one who was once a zealous worker in the Lord's Vineyard, I challenge you to deny that in the great *Papalangi* countries the system works."

Ieremia could not deny, and his fingers played nervously with the fastening of the basket on his knees.

"You see, it is as I have said," Cornelius continued. "Ieremia agrees that it is so. Therefore, I ask you, all good people of Fitu-Iva, if a system is good for the *Papalangi* countries, why is it not good for Fitu-Iva?"

"It is not the same!" Ieremia cried. "The paper of Feathers of the Sun is different from the paper of the great countries."

That Cornelius had been prepared for this was evident. He held up a Fitu-Ivan note that was recognized by all.

"What is that?" he demanded.

"Paper, mere paper," was Ieremia's reply.

"And that?"

This time Cornelius held up a United States dollar bill.

"It is the paper money of the Americans," he explained to the Council, at the same time extending it for Ieremia to examine. "Is it not true, Ieremia, that it is paper money of the Americans?"

Ieremia nodded reluctantly.

"You have said that the paper money of Fitu-Iva was paper, now how about this of the Americans? What is it? . . . You must answer like a true man. . . . All wait for your answer, Ieremia."

"It is—it is——" the puzzled Ieremia began, then spluttered helplessly.

"Paper, mere paper," Cornelius concluded for him, imitating his halting utterance.

Conviction sat on the faces of all. The King clapped his hands admiringly and murmured, "It is most clear, very clear."

"You see, he himself acknowledges it." Assured triumph was in Deasy's voice and bearing. "He knows of no difference. There is no difference. 'Tis the very image of money. 'Tis money itself."

In the meantime Grief was whispering in Ieremia's ear, who nodded and again began to speak.

"But it is well known to all the *Papalangi* that the United States Government will pay coin money for the paper."

Deasy's victory was now absolute. He held aloft a Fitu-Ivan note.

"Is is not so written on this paper as well?"

Again Grief whispered.

"That Fitu-Iva will pay coin money?" asked Ieremia.

"It is so written."

A third time Grief prompted.

"On demand?" asked Ieremia.

"On demand," Cornelius assured him.

"Then I demand coin money now," said Ieremia, drawing a small package of notes from the pouch at his girdle.

Cornelius scanned the package with a quick, estimating eye.

"Very well," he agreed. "I shall give you coin money now. How much?"

"And we will see the system work," the King proclaimed, partaking in his Chancellor's triumph.

"You have heard!—He will give coin money now!" Ieremia cried in a loud voice to the assemblage.

At the same time he plunged both hands in the basket and drew forth many packages of Fitu-Ivan notes. And it was noticed that a peculiar odor was adrift about the Council.

"I have here," Ieremia announced. "five thousand one hundred forty-three dollars and ten cents. Here is a sack to put the coin money in."

Cornelius recoiled. He had not expected such a sum, and everywhere about the Council his uneasy eyes showed him chiefs and talking men drawing out bundles of notes. The army, its two months' pay in its hands, pressed forward to the edge of the Council, while behind it the populace, with more money, invaded the compound.

" 'Tis a run on the bank you've precipitated," he said reproachfully to Grief.

"Here is the sack to put the coin money in," Ieremia urged.

"It must be postponed," Cornelius said desperately. " 'Tis not in banking hours."

Ieremia flourished a package of money. "Nothing of banking hours is written here. It says *on demand,* and I now demand."

"Let them come to-morrow, O Tui Tulifau," Cornelius appealed to the King. "They shall be paid to-morrow."

Tui Tulifau hesitated, but his spouse glared at him, her brawny arm tensing as the fist doubled into a redoubtable knot. Tui Tulifau tried to look away, but failed. He cleared his throat nervously.

"We will see the system work," he decreed. "The people have come far."

" 'Tis good money you're asking me to pay out," Deasy muttered in a low voice to the King.

Sepeli caught what he said, and grunted so savagely as to startle the King, who involuntarily shrank away from her.

"Forget not the pig," Grief whispered to Ieremia, who immediately stood up.

With a sweeping gesture he stilled the babel of voices that was beginning to rise.

"It was an ancient and honorable custom of Fitu-Iva," he said, "that when a man was proved a notorious evildoer his joints were broken with a club and he was staked out at low water to be fed upon alive by the sharks. Unfortunately, that day is past. Nevertheless another ancient and honorable custom remains with us. You all know what it is. When a man is a proven thief and liar he shall be struck with a dead pig."

His right hand went into the basket, and, despite the lack of spectacles, the dead pig that came into view landed accurately on Deasy's neck. With such force was it thrown that the Chancellor, in his sitting position, toppled over sidewise. Before he could recover, Sepeli, with an agility unexpected of a woman who weighed two hundred and sixty pounds, had sprung across to him. One hand clutched his shirt collar, the other hand brandished the pig, and amid the vast uproar of a delighted kingdom she royally swatted him.

There remained nothing for Tui Tulifau but to put a good face on his favorite's disgrace, and his mountainous fat lay back on the mats and shook in a gale of Gargantuan laughter.

When Sepeli dropped both pig and Chancellor, a talking man from the windward coast picked up the carcass. Cornelius was on his feet and running, when the pig caught him on the legs and tripped him. The people and the army, with shouts and laughter, joined in the sport. Twist and dodge as he would, everywhere the ex-Chancellor of the Exchequer was met or overtaken by the flying pig. He scuttled like a frightened rabbit in and out among the avocados and the palms. No hand was laid upon him, and his tormentors made way before him, but ever they pursued, and ever the pig flew as fast as hands could pick it up.

As the chase died away down the Broom Road, Grief led the traders to the Royal Treasury, and the day was well over ere the last Fitu-Ivan bank note had been redeemed with coin.

Through the mellow cool of twilight a man paddled out from a clump of jungle to the *Cantani*. It was a leaky and abandoned dugout, and he paddled slowly, desisting from time to time in order to bale. The Kanaka sailors giggled gleefully as he came alongside and painfully drew himself over the rail. He was bedraggled and filthy, and seemed half-dazed.

"Could I speak a word with you, Mr. Grief?" he asked sadly and humbly.

"Sit to leeward and farther away," Grief answered. "A little farther away. That's better."

Cornelius sat down on the rail and held his head in both his hands.

" 'Tis right," he said. "I'm as fragrant as a recent battle-field. My head aches to burstin'. My neck is fair broken. The teeth are loose in my jaws. There's nests of hornets buzzin' in my ears. My medulla oblongata is dislocated. I've been through earthquake and pestilence, and the heavens have rained pigs." He paused with a sigh that ended in a groan. " 'Tis a vision of terrible death. One that the poets never dreamed. To be eaten by rats, or boiled in oil, or pulled apart by wild horses—that would be unpleasant. But to be beaten to death with a dead pig!" He shuddered at the awfulness of it. "Sure it transcends the human imagination."

Captain Boig sniffed audibly, moved his canvas chair farther to windward, and sat down again.

"I hear you're runnin' over to Yap, Mr. Grief," Cornelius went on. "An' two things I'm wantin' to beg of you: a passage—an' a nip of that whisky I refused the night you landed."

Grief clapped his hands for the native steward and ordered soap and towels.

"Go for'ard, Cornelius, and take a scrub first," he said. "The steward will bring you a pair of dungarees and a shirt.

And by the way, before you go, how was it we found more coin in the Treasury than paper you had issued?"

" 'Twas the stake of my own I'd brought with me for the adventure."

"We've decided to charge the demurrage and other expenses and loss to Tui Tulifau," Grief said. "So the balance we found will be turned over to you. But two and half dollars must be deducted."

"For what?"

"Do you think dead pigs grow on trees? The sum of two fifty for that pig is entered in the accounts."

Cornelius bowed his assent with a shudder.

"Sure it's grateful I am it wasn't a three seventy-five pig or a five-dollar one."

CHAPTER 7 · *The Pearls of Parlay*

T HE KANAKA helmsman put the wheel down, and the *Malahini* slipped into the eye of the wind and righted to an even keel. Her headsails emptied, there was a rat-tat of reef points and a quick shifting of boom tackles, and she heeled over and filled away on the other tack. Though it was early morning and the wind brisk, the five men who lounged on the poop deck were scantily clad. David Grief and his guest, Gregory Mulhall, an Englishman, were still in pajamas, their naked feet thrust into Chinese slippers. The captain and mate were in thin undershirts and unstarched duck pants, while the supercargo still held in his hands the undershirt he was reluctant to put on. The sweat stood out on his forehead, and he thrust his bare chest thirstily into a wind that did not cool.

"Pretty muggy for a breeze like this," he complained.

"What's it doing around in the west? That's what I want to know," was Grief's contribution to the general griping.

"It won't last—it ain't been there long," said Hermann, the Dutch mate. "She is been chop around all night—five minutes here, ten minutes there, one hour somewhere other quarter."

"Something makin', something makin'," Captain Warfield croaked, spreading his bushy beard with the fingers of both hands and shoving the thatch of his chin into the breeze in a vain search for coolness. "Weather's been crazy for a fortnight. Haven't had the proper trades in three weeks. Everything's mixed up. Barometer was pumping at sunset last night, and it's pumping now, though the weathermen say that don't mean anything. All the same, I've got a prejudice against seeing it pump. Gets on my nerves, sort of. She was pumping that way the time we lost the *Lancaster*. I was only an apprentice, but I can remember that well enough. Brand new, four-masted steel ship; first voyage; broke the old man's heart. He'd been forty years in the Company. Just faded away and died the next year."

Despite the wind and the early hour, the heat was suffocating. The wind whispered, but did not deliver, coolness. It might have blown off the Sahara, save for the extreme humidity with which it was laden. There was no fog or mist, nor hint of fog or mist, yet the dimness of distance produced the impression. There were no defined clouds, yet so thickly were the heavens covered by a messy cloudpall that the sun failed to shine through.

"Ready about!" Captain Warfield ordered sharply.

The breechclouted Kanaka sailors moved quickly to the headsheets and boom tackles.

"Hard alee!"

The helmsman ran the spokes over with no hint of gentling, and the *Malahini* darted prettily into the wind and about.

"Jove! She's a witch!" was Mulhall's appreciation. "I didn't know you South Sea traders sailed yachts."

"She was a Gloucester fisherman originally," Grief explained. "The Gloucester boats are *all* yachts when it comes to build, rig, and sailing."

"But you were heading right in—why didn't you hold course?" came the Englishman's criticism.

"Try it, Captain Warfield," Grief suggested. "Show him what a lagoon entrance is like on a strong ebb."

"Close-and-by!" the captain ordered.

"Close-and-by," a Kanaka repeated, easing half a spoke.

The *Malahini* laid squarely into the narrow passage which was the lagoon entrance of a large, long and narrow oval of an atoll. The atoll was shaped as if three atolls, in the course of building, had collided and coalesced but failed to rear their partition walls. Coconut palms grew in spots on the circle of sand, and there were many gaps where the sand was too close to sea level for coconuts, and through which could be seen the protected lagoon where the water lay flat like the unruffled surface of a mirror. Many square miles of water were in the irregular lagoon, all of which surged out on the ebb through the one narrow channel. So narrow was the channel and so large the outflow of water that the passage was more like the rapids of a river than the mere tidal entrance to an atoll. The water boiled and whirled and swirled and drove outward in a white foam of stiff, serrated waves. Each heave and blow of the upstanding waves of the current on her bows swung the *Malahini* off the straight lead and wedged her as with wedges of steel toward the side of the passage. She was only part way in when her closeness to the coral edge compelled her to go about. On the opposite tack, broadside to the current, she swept seaward with the current's speed.

"Now's the time for that expensive new engine of yours," Grief jeered good-naturedly.

The engine was a sore point with Captain Warfield. He had begged and badgered for it, until in the end Grief had given his consent.

"It will pay for itself yet," the captain retorted. "You wait and see. It beats insurance—and you know the underwriters won't stand for insurance in the Tuamotus."

Grief pointed to a small cutter beating up astern of them on the same course.

"I'll still bet that little *Nuhiva* beats us in."

"Sure," Captain Warfield agreed. "She's *over*powered. We're like a liner alongside of her, but we've only got forty horsepower. She's got ten horse, and she's a little skimming dish. She could skate across the froth of hell—but just the same she can't buck this current. It's running ten knots right now."

And at the rate of ten knots, buffeted and rolling jerkily, the *Malahini* went out to sea with the tide.

"She'll slacken in half an hour—then we'll make headway," Captain Warfield said, with an irritation explained by his next words. "He has no right to call it Parlay. It's down on the Admiralty charts, and the French charts, too, as Hikihoho. Bougainville discovered it and named it from the natives."

"What does the name matter?" the supercargo demanded, pausing with his arms shoved into the sleeves of the undershirt. "There it is, right under our nose, and old Parlay is there with the pearls."

"Who see them pearl?" Hermann queried, looking from one to another.

The supercargo turned to the steersman: "Tai-Hotauri, what about old Parlay's pearls?"

The Kanaka, pleased and self-conscious, took and gave a spoke.

"My brother dive for Parlay three, four month, and he make much talk about pearl. Hikihoho very good place for pearl."

"And the pearl buyers have never got him to part with a pearl," the captain broke in.

"They say he had a hatful all ready for Armande when he sailed for Tahiti," the supercargo carried on the tale. "That's fifteen years ago, and he's been adding to it ever since—storing the shell as well. Everybody's seen *that*—hundreds of tons of it. They say the lagoon's fished clean now. Maybe that's why he's announced the auction."

"If he really sells, this will be the biggest year's output of pearls in the Tuamotus," Grief said.

"I say, now!" Mulhall burst. "Who's the old beachcomber anyway? What are all these pearls? Why so secretive about it?"

"Hikihoho belongs to old Parlay," the supercargo answered. "He's got a fortune in pearls, saved up for years and years, and he sent word out weeks ago that he'd auction them off to buyers tomorrow. See those schooners' masts sticking up inside the lagoon?"

"Eight I see," said Hermann.

"What do you think they're all doing in a dinky atoll like this," the supercargo went on. "There isn't a schooner-load of copra a year in the place. They've come for the auction. That's why *we're* here. That's why the little *Nuhiva's* bumping along astern there, though what *she* can buy is beyond me. Narii Herring owns and runs her, and his only assets are his nerve, his debts, and his whiskey bills. He's a genius in such things. He owes so much that there isn't a merchant in Papeete who isn't interested in his welfare. They go out of their way to throw work in his way. They've got to, and a soft touch it is for Narii. Now I owe nobody. What's the result? If I fell down in a fit on the beach they'd let me lie there and die. They wouldn't lose anything. But Narii Herring?—what *wouldn't* they do if he fell in a fit? Their best wouldn't be too good for him. They've got too much money tied up in him to let him lie. They'd take him into their homes and hand nurse him like a brother. Let me tell you, honesty in paying bills ain't what it's cracked up to be."

"What's this Narii chap got to do with it?" was the Englishman's demand. And, turning to Grief, he said, "What's all this pearl nonsense? Begin at the beginning."

"You'll have to help me," Grief told the others, as he began. "Old Parlay is a character. From what I've seen of him I believe he's mildly insane. Anyway, here's the story: Parlay's a full-blooded Frenchman. He told me once that he came from Paris. His accent is the true Parisian. He arrived down here in the old days. Went to trading and all the rest.

That's how he got in on Hikihoho. Came in trading when trading was the real thing. About a hundred miserable Tuamotans lived on the island. He married the queen—native fashion. When she died, everything was his. Measles came through, and there weren't more than a dozen survivors. He fed them, and worked them, and was king. Now before the queen died she gave birth to a girl. That's Armande. When she was three he sent her to the convent at Papeete. When she was seven or eight he sent her to France. You begin to glimpse the situation. The best and most aristocratic school in France was none too good for the only daughter of a Tuamotan island king and capitalist, and the French draw no color line. She was educated like a princess, and she accepted herself in much the same way. Also, she thought she was white.

"Now comes the tragedy. The old man had always been cranky and erratic, and he'd played the despot on Hikihoho so long that he'd got the idea in his head that there was nothing unusual about the princess. When Armande was eighteen he sent for her. He'd built the big house on Hikihoho, and a peach of a cottage in Papeete. She was to arrive on the mail boat from New Zealand, and he sailed in his schooner to meet her at Papeete. And he might have carried the situation off, despite the wagging tongues of Papeete, if it hadn't been for the hurricane. That was the year, wasn't it, when Manu-Huhi was swept and eleven hundred drowned?"

The others nodded, and Captain Warfield said: "I was in the *Magpie* that blow, and we went ashore, all hands and the cook, *Magpie* and all, a quarter of a mile into the coconuts at the head of Taiohae Bay—and it a supposedly hurricane-proof harbor."

"Well," Grief continued, "old Parlay got caught in the same blow. He had to jack up his schooner and build half a mile of ways before he could get her back into the sea. He arrived in Papeete with his hatful of pearls three weeks too late.

"And in the meantime there was Armande at Papeete. Nobody called on her. She did, French fashion, make the initial calls on the Governor and the port doctor. They peered out at her, but neither of their hen-wives was at home to her nor returned the call. She was out of caste, without caste, though she had never dreamed it, and that was the gentle way they broke the information to her. There was a gay young lieutenant on a French cruiser. He lost his heart to her, but not his head. You can imagine the shock to this young woman, refined, beautiful, raised like an aristocrat, pampered with the best of old France that money could buy. You can guess the end." He shrugged his shoulders. "There was a Japanese servant in the cottage. He saw it. Said she did it with the proper spirit of the Samurai. Took a stiletto—no thrust, no drive, no wild rush for annihilation—took the stiletto, placed the point carefully against her heart, and with both hands, slowly and steadily, pressed home.

"Old Parlay arrived after that with his pearls. There was one of them, they say, worth twelve thousand dollars. Peter Gee saw it, and told me he offered that much for it. The old man went clean off for a while. They had him strait jacketed in the Colonial Club two days——"

"His wife's uncle, an old Tuamotan, cut him out of the jacket and turned him loose," the supercargo corroborated.

"And then old Parlay proceeded to eat things up," Grief went on. "Pumped three bullets into that crumb of a lieu-tenant——"

"Who lay in sick bay for three months," Captain War-field contributed.

"Flung a glass of wine in the Governor's face; fought a duel with the port doctor; beat up his native servants; wrecked the hospital; broke two ribs and the collarbone of a man nurse, and escaped; and went down to his schooner, a gun in each hand, daring the chief of police and all the gendarmes to arrest him, and sailed for Hikihoho. They say he's never left the island since."

The supercargo nodded. "That was fifteen years ago, and he's never budged."

"Just added to his pearls," said the captain. "He's a blithering old lunatic. Makes my flesh creep. He's a regular Finn."

"What's that?" Mulhall inquired.

"Bosses the weather—that's what the natives believe, at any rate. Ask Tai-Hotauri there. Hey, Tai-Hotauri! What you think old Parlay do along weather?"

"Just the same one big weather devil," came the Kanaka's answer. "I know. He want big blow, he make big blow. He want no wind, no wind come."

"A regular old sorcerer," said Mulhall.

"No good luck them pearl," Tai-Hotauri blurted out, rolling his head ominously. "He say he sell. Plenty schooner come. Then he make big hurricane, everybody finish, you see. All native men say so."

"It's hurricane season now anyway," Captain Warfield laughed morosely. "They're not far wrong. It's making for something right now. I'd feel better if the *Malahini* was a thousand miles away from here."

"Parlay *is* a bit mad," Grief concluded. "I've tried to get his point of view. It's—well, it's mixed. For eighteen years he centered everything on Armande. Half the time he believes she's still alive, not yet back from France. That's one of the reasons he held on to the pearls. And all the time he hates white men. He never forgets they killed her, though a great deal of the time he forgets she's dead. Hello! Where's your wind?"

The sails bellied emptily overhead, and Captain Warfield grunted his disgust. Intolerable as the heat had been, in the absence of wind it was almost overpowering. The sweat oozed out on all their faces, and now one and again another drew deep breaths, involuntarily questing for more air.

"Here she comes again—an eight point haul! Boom tackles across! Jump!"

The Kanakas sprang to the captain's orders, and for five minutes the schooner laid directly into the passage and even gained on the current. Again the breeze fell flat, then puffed from the old quarter, compelling a shift back of sheets and tackles.

"Here comes the *Nuhiva*," Grief said. "She's got her engine on. Look at her skim."

"All ready?" the captain asked the engineer, a Portuguese half-caste, whose head and shoulders protruded from the small hatch just for'ard of the cabin, and who wiped the sweat from his face with a bunch of greasy waste.

"Sure," he replied.

"Then let her go."

The engineer disappeared into his den, and a moment later the exhaust muffler coughed and spluttered overside. But the schooner could not hold her head. The little cutter made three feet to her two and was quickly alongside and forging ahead. Only natives were on her deck, and the man steering waved his hand in derisive greeting and farewell.

"That's Narii Herring," Grief told Mulhall. "The big fellow at the wheel—the nerviest and most conscienceless scoundrel in the Tuamotus."

Five minutes later a cry of joy from their own Kanakas centered all eyes on the *Nuhiva*. Her engine had broken down and they were overtaking her. The *Malahini's* sailors sprang into the rigging and jeered as they went by; the little cutter heeled over by the wind with a bone in her teeth, going backward on the tide.

"Some engine—ours," Grief approved, as the lagoon opened before them and the course was changed across to the anchorage.

Captain Warfield was visibly cheered, though he merely grunted, "It'll pay for itself, never fear."

The *Malahini* ran well into the center of the little fleet ere she found swinging room to anchor.

"There's Isaacs on the *Dolly*," Grief observed, with a hand wave of greeting. "And Peter Gee's on the *Roberta*. Couldn't keep him away from a pearl sale like this. And there's Francini on the *Cactus*. They're all here, all the buyers. Old Parlay will surely get a price."

"They haven't repaired the engine yet," Captain Warfield grumbled gleefully.

He was looking across the lagoon to where only the *Nuhiva's* sails showed through the sparse coconuts.

The house of Parlay was a big two-story frame affair, built of California lumber, with a galvanized iron roof. So disproportionate was it to the slender ring of the atoll that it stood out on the sand strip like some monstrous excrescence.

They of the *Malahini* paid the courtesy visit ashore immediately after anchoring. Other captains and buyers were in the big room, examining the pearls that were to be auctioned next day. Tuamotan servants, natives of Hikihoho and relatives of the owner, moved about dispensing whiskey and absinthe. And through the curious company moved Parlay himself, cackling and sneering, the withered wreck of what had once been a tall and powerful man. His eyes were deep sunken and feverish, his cheeks fallen in and cavernous. The hair of his head seemed to have come out in patches, and his mustache and beard had shed in the same lopsided way.

"Jove!" Mulhall muttered under his breath. "Long legged, burnt out, baked, and fire-crackled. And mangy! No wonder he crooks his head to one side. He's got to keep his balance."

"Goin' to have a blow," was the old man's greeting to Grief. "You must think a lot of pearls to come on a day like this."

"They're worth going to hell for," Grief laughed genially back, running his eyes over the display covering the surface of the table.

"Other men have already made that journey for them," old Parlay cackled. "See this one!" He pointed to a large perfect pearl the size of a small walnut that lay apart on a piece of chamois. "They offered me twelve thousand dollars for that in Tahiti. They'll bid as much and more for it tomorrow—if they aren't blown away. That pearl was found by my cousin, my cousin by marriage. He was a native, you see. Also, he was a thief. He hid it. It was mine. His cousin, who was also my cousin—we're all related here—killed him for it and fled away in a boat to Noo-Nau. I pursued, but the chief of Noo-Nau had killed him for it before I got there. Yes, there are many dead men represented on the table there.

Have a drink, Captain. Your face is not familiar. You are new in the islands?"

"Captain Robinson of the *Roberta*," Grief said, introducing them.

In the meantime Mulhall had shaken hands with Peter Gee.

"I never fancied there were so many pearls in the world," Mulhall said.

"Nor have I ever seen so many together at one time," Peter Gee admitted.

"What should they be worth?"

"Two hundred fifty or three hundred thousand dollars—and that's to us buyers. In Paris——" He shrugged his shoulders and lifted his eyebrows at the fantastic nature of the sum.

Mulhall wiped the sweat from his eyes. All were sweating profusely and breathing hard. There was no ice in the drink served, and whiskey and absinthe went down lukewarm.

"Yes," Parlay was cackling. "Many dead men lie on the table there. I know those pearls, all of them. You see those three! Perfectly matched, aren't they? A diver from Easter Island got them for me inside a week. Next week a shark got him; took his arm off and blood poison finished the business. And that big baroque there—nothing much—if I'm offered four dollars for it tomorrow I'll be in luck; it came out of twenty-two fathoms of water. The man was from Raratonga. He broke all diving records. And he burst his lungs at the same time with the 'bends,' for he died in two hours. He died screaming. They could hear him for miles. He was the most powerful native I ever saw. Half a dozen of my divers have died of the 'bends.' And more men will die, more men will die."

"Oh, lay off croaking, Parlay," chided one of the captains. "It ain't going to blow."

"If I was a strong man, I couldn't get up hook and get out fast enough," the old man retorted in the falsetto of age. "Not if I was a strong man with the taste for wine yet in my mouth. But not you. You'll all stay. I wouldn't advise you if I thought you'd go. You can't drive buzzards away from carrion. Have another drink, my brave sailormen. Well, well—what men will dare for a few little oyster drops! There they are, the beauties! Auction tomorrow at ten sharp. Old Parlay's selling out, and the buzzards are gathering—old Parlay who was a stronger man in his day than any of them and who will see most of them dead yet."

"Isn't he a vile old beast!" the supercargo of the *Malahini* whispered to Peter Gee.

"What if she does blow?" said the captain of the *Dolly*. "Hikihoho's never been swept."

"The more reason she will be, then," Captain Warfield answered back. "I wouldn't trust her."

"Who's croaking now?" Grief reproved.

"I'd hate to lose that new engine before it paid for itself," Captain Warfield replied gloomily.

With astonishing nimbleness, Parlay skipped across the crowded room to the barometer on the wall.

"Take a look, brave sailormen!" he cried exultantly.

The man nearest read the glass. The sobering effect showed plainly on his face.

"It's dropped ten," was all he said, yet every face went anxious, and every man looked as if he was ready to start out the door.

"Listen!" Parlay commanded.

In the silence the outer surf seemed to have become unusually loud. There was a great rumbling roar.

"A big sea beginning to set," some one said; and there was a movement to the windows.

Through the sparse coconuts they gazed seaward. An orderly succession of huge smooth seas was rolling down upon the coral shore. For some minutes they gazed on the strange sight and talked in low voices, and in those few minutes it was plain to all that the waves were increasing in size. It was uncanny, this rising sea in a dead calm, and their voices unconsciously sank lower. Old Parlay shocked them with his abrupt cackle.

"There is yet time to get away to sea, brave gentlemen. You can tow across the lagoon with your whaleboats."

"It's all right, old man," said Darling, mate of the *Cactus* and a stalwart youngster of twenty-five. "The blow's to the south'ard and passing on. We'll not get a whiff of it."

An air of relief went through the room. Conversations recommenced, and the voices became louder. Several of the buyers even went back to the table to continue examining the pearls.

Parlay's shrill cackle rose higher.

"That's right," he encouraged. "If the world was coming to an end you'd go on buying."

"We'll buy these tomorrow just the same," Isaacs assured him.

"Then you'll be doing your buying in hell."

The chorus of incredulous laughter incensed the old man. He turned fiercely on Darling.

"Since when have children like you any knowledge of

storms? And who is the man who has plotted the hurricane courses of the Tuamotus? In what books will you find it? I sailed the Tuamotus before the oldest of you drew breath. I know. To the eastward the paths of the hurricanes are on so wide a circle they make a straight line. To the westward here they make a sharp curve. Remember your chart. How did it happen the hurricane of '91 swept Auri and Hiolau? The curve, my brave boy, the curve! In an hour, or two or three at most, will come the wind. Listen to that!"

A vast rumbling crash shook the coral foundations of the atoll. The house quivered. The native servants, with bottles of whiskey and absinthe in their hands, shrank together as if for protection and stared with fear through the windows at the mighty wash of the giant wave lapping far up the beach to the corner of a copra shed.

Parlay looked at the barometer, giggled, and leered around at his guests. Captain Warfield strode across to see.

"29.75," he read. "She's gone down five more. By God! The old devil's right. She's a-coming, and I, for one, am going aboard."

"It's growing dark," Isaacs half whispered.

"Jove! it's like a stage," Mulhall said to Grief, looking at his watch. "Ten o'clock in the morning, and it's like twilight. Down go the lights for the tragedy. Where's the slow music!"

In answer, another rumbling crash shook the atoll and the house. Almost in panic the company started for the door. In the dim light their sweaty faces appeared ghastly. Isaacs panted asthmatically in the suffocating heat.

"What's your haste?" Parlay chuckled and scoffed at his departing guests. "A last drink, brave gentlemen." No one noticed him. As they took the shell-bordered path to the beach he stuck his head out the door and called, "Don't forget, gentlemen, at ten tomorrow old Parlay sells his pearls."

On the beach a curious scene took place. Whaleboat after whaleboat was hurriedly manned and shoved off. It had grown still darker. The stagnant calm continued, and the sand shook under their feet with each buffet of the sea on the outer shore. Narii Herring walked leisurely along the sand. He grinned at the very evident haste of the captains and buyers. With him were three of his Kanakas, and also Tai-Hotauri.

"Get into the boat and take an oar," Captain Warfield ordered the latter.

Tai-Hotauri came over jauntily, while Narii Herring and his three Kanakas paused and looked on from forty feet away.

"I work no more for you, skipper," Tai-Hotauri said insolently and loudly. But his face belied his words, for he was guilty of a prodigious wink. "Fire me, skipper," he huskily whispered, with a second significant wink.

Captain Warfield took the cue and proceeded to do some acting himself. He raised his fist and his voice.

"Get into that boat," he thundered, "or I'll knock seven bells out of you!"

The Kanaka drew back truculently, and Grief stepped between to placate his captain.

"I go to work on the *Nuhiva*," Tai-Hotauri said, rejoining the other group.

"Come back here!" the captain threatened.

"He's a free man, skipper," Narii Herring spoke up. "He's sailed with me in the past, and he's sailing again, that's all."

"Come on, we must get on board," Grief urged. "Look how dark it's getting."

Captain Warfield gave in, but as the boat shoved off he stood up in the sternsheets and shook his fist ashore.

"I'll settle with you yet, Narii," he cried. "You're the only skipper around that steals other men's sailors." He sat down, and in lowered voice queried: "Now what's Tai-Hotauri up to? He's on to something, but what is it?"

As the boat came alongside the *Malahini*, Hermann's anxious face greeted them over the rail.

"Bottom fall out from barometer," he announced. "She's goin' to blow. I got starboard anchor overhaul."

"Overhaul the big one, too," Captain Warfield ordered, taking charge. "And here, some of you, hoist in this boat. Lower her down to the deck and lash her, bottom up."

Men were busy at work on the decks of all the schooners. There was a great clanking of chains being overhauled, and now one craft after another hove in, veered, and dropped a second anchor. Like the *Malahini*, those that had third anchors were preparing to drop them when the wind showed from what quarter it was to blow.

The roar of the big surf continually grew, though the lagoon lay in the mirror-like calm. There was no sign of life where Parlay's big house perched on the sand. Boat and copra sheds and the sheds where the shell was stored were deserted.

"For two cents I'd up anchor and get out," Grief said. "I'd do it anyway if it were open sea. But those chains of

atolls to the north and east have us pocketed. We've a better chance right here. What do you think, Captain Warfield?"

"I agree with you, though a lagoon is no millpond for
riding it out. I wonder where she's going to start from? Hello!
There goes one of Parlay's copra sheds."

They could see the grass-thatched shed lift and collapse,
while a froth of foam cleared the crest of the sand and ran
down to the lagoon.

"Breached across!" Mulhall exclaimed. "That's something
for a starter. There she comes again!"

The wreck of the shed was now flung up and left on the
sand-crest. A third wave buffeted it into fragments which
washed down the slope toward the lagoon.

"If she blow I would be cooler yet," Hermann grunted.
"No longer can I breathe. It is damn hot. I am dry like a
stove."

He chopped open a drinking coconut with his heavy sheath
knife and drained the contents. The rest of them followed his
example, pausing once to watch one of Parlay's shell sheds go
down in ruin. The barometer now registered 29.50.

"Must be pretty close to the center of the low-pressure
area," Grief remarked cheerfully. "Were you ever through
the eye of a hurricane before? It will be an experience, Mulhall. From the speed the barometer's dropped, it's going to be
a big one."

Captain Warfield groaned, and all eyes drew to him. He
was looking through the glasses down the length of the
lagoon to the southeast.

"There she comes," he said quietly.

They did not need glasses to see. A flying film, strangely

marked, seemed drawing over the surface of the lagoon. Abreast of it along the atoll, traveling with equal speed, was a stiff bending of the coconut palms and a blur of flying leaves. The front of the wind on the water was a solid, sharply defined strip of dark-colored, wind-vexed water. In advance of this strip, like skirmishers, were flashes of wind flaws. Behind this strip, a quarter of a mile in width, was a strip of what seemed glassy calm. Next came another dark strip of wind, and behind that, the lagoon was all crisping, boiling whiteness.

"What is that calm streak?" Mulhall asked.

"Calm," Warfield answered.

"But it travels as fast as the wind," was the other's objection.

"It has to, or it would be overtaken and there wouldn't be any calm. It's a double-header. I saw a big squall like that off Savaii once. A regular double-header. Smash! it hit us, lulled to nothing, and then smashed us a second time. Stand by and hold on! Here she is on top of us! Look at the *Roberta*!"

The *Roberta*, lying nearest to the wind at slack chains, was swept off broadside like a straw. Then her chains brought her up, bow on to the wind, with an astonishing jerk. Schooner after schooner, the *Malahini* with them, was now sweeping away with the first gust and fetching up on taut chains. Mulhall and several of the Kanakas were taken off their feet when the *Malahini* jerked to her anchors.

And then there was no wind. The flying calm streak had reached them. Grief lighted a match, and the unshielded flame burned without flickering in the still air. A very dim twilight prevailed. The cloudy sky, lowering as it had been for hours, seemed now to have descended completely down upon the sea.

The *Roberta* tightened to her chains when the second head of the hurricane hit, as did schooner after schooner in swift succession. The sea, white with fury, boiled in tiny, spitting wavelets. The deck of the *Malahini* vibrated under the men's feet. The taut-stretched halyards beat a tattoo against the masts, and all the rigging, as if smote by some mighty hand, set up a wild thrumming. It was impossible to face the wind and breathe. Mulhall, crouching with the others behind the shelter of the cabin, discovered this, and his lungs were filled in an instant with so great a volume of driven air which he could not expel that he nearly strangled before he could turn his head away.

"It's incredible," he gasped, but no one heard him.

Hermann and several Kanakas were crawling for'ard on hands and knees to let go the third anchor. Grief touched Captain Warfield and pointed to the *Roberta*. She was dragging down upon them. Warfield put his mouth to Grief's ear and shouted:

"We're dragging, too!"

Grief sprang to the wheel and put it hard over, veering the *Malahini* to port. The third anchor took hold, and the *Roberta* went by, stern-first, a dozen yards away. They waved their hands to Peter Gee and Captain Robinson, who, with a number of sailors, were at work at the bow.

"He's knocking out the shackles!" Grief shouted. "Going to chance the passage! Got to! Anchors skating!"

"We're holding now!" came Captain Warfield's answering shout. "There goes the *Cactus* down on the *Misi*. That settles them!"

The *Misi* had been holding, but the added windage of the *Cactus* was too much, and the entangled schooners slid away across the boiling white. Their men could be seen chopping and fighting to get them apart. The *Roberta*, cleared of her anchors, with a patch of tarpaulin set for'ard, was heading for the passage at the northwestern end of the lagoon. They saw her make it and drive out to sea. But the *Misi* and *Cactus*, unable to get clear of each other, went ashore on the atoll half a mile from the passage.

The wind merely increased and continued to increase. To face the full blast of it required all one's strength. Several minutes of crawling on deck against it tired a man to exhaustion. Hermann with his Kanakas plodded steadily, lashing and making secure, putting ever more gaskets on the sails. The wind ripped and tore the thin undershirts from their backs. They moved slowly, as if their bodies weighed tons, never releasing a handhold until another had been secured. Loose ends of rope stood out stiffly horizontal, frazzled, and blew away.

Mulhall touched one and then another and pointed to the shore. The grass sheds had disappeared, and Parlay's house rocked drunkenly. Because the wind blew lengthwise along the atoll, the house had been sheltered by the miles of coconut trees. But the big seas, breaking across from outside, were undermining it and hammering it to pieces. Already tilted down the slope of sand, its end was imminent. Here and there in the coconut trees people had lashed themselves. The trees did not sway or thresh about. Bent over rigidly from the wind, they remained in that position and vibrated monstrously. Underneath, across the sand, surged the white spume of the breakers.

A big sea was likewise making down the length of the lagoon. It had plenty of room to kick up in the ten-mile stretch from the windward rim of the atoll, and all the schooners were bucking and plunging into it. The *Malahini* had begun shoving her bow and fo'c'sle head under the bigger ones, and at times her waist was filled rail-high with water.

"Now's the time for your engine!" Grief bellowed; and Captain Warfield, crawling over to where the engineer lay, shouted emphatic commands.

Once the engine was going full speed ahead, the *Malahini* behaved better. While she continued to ship seas over her bow, she was not jerked down so fiercely by her anchors. Nevertheless, she was unable to get any slack in the chains. The best her forty horsepower could do was to ease the strain.

Still the wind increased. The little *Nuhiva*, lying abreast of the *Malahini* and closer in to the beach, her engine still unrepaired and her captain ashore, was having a bad time of it. She buried herself so frequently and so deeply that they wondered each time if she could clear herself of the water. At three in the afternoon, buried by a second sea before she could free herself of the preceding one, she did not come up.

Mulhall looked at Grief.

"Burst in her hatches," was the bellowed answer.

Captain Warfield pointed to the *Winifred*, a little schooner plunging and burying outside of them, and shouted in Grief's ear. His voice came in patches of dim words, with intervals of silence when whisked away by the roaring wind.

"Rotten little tub . . . Anchors hold . . . But how *she* holds together . . . Old as the Ark——"

An hour later Hermann pointed to her. Her for'ard bitts, foremast, and most of her bow were gone, having been jerked out of her by her anchors. She swung broadside, rolling in the trough and settling by the head, and in this plight was swept away to leeward.

Five vessels now remained, and of them the *Malahini* was the only one with an engine. Fearing either the *Nuhiva's* or the *Winifred's* fate, two of them followed the *Roberta's* example, knocking out the chain shackles and running for the passage. The *Dolly* was first, but her tarpaulin carried away, and she went to destruction on the lee rim of the atoll near the *Misi* and the *Cactus*. Undeterred, the *Moana* let go and followed—with the same result.

"Pretty good engine, eh?" Captain Warfield yelled to his owner.

Grief put out his hand and shook. "She's paying for herself!" he yelled back. "The wind's shifting around to the south'ard, and we ought to lie easier!"

Slowly and steadily, but with ever increasing velocity, the wind veered around to the south and the southwest, till the three schooners that were left pointed directly in toward the beach. The wreck of Parlay's house was picked up, hurled into the lagoon, and blown out upon them. Passing the *Malahini*, it crashed into the *Papara*, lying a quarter of a mile astern. There was wild work for'ard on her, and in a quarter of an hour the house went clear, but it had taken the *Papara's* foremast and bowsprit with it.

Inshore, on their port bow, lay the *Tahaa*, slim and yacht-like, but excessively oversparred. Her anchors still held, but her captain, finding no abatement in the wind, proceeded to reduce windage by chopping down his masts.

"Pretty good engine that," Grief congratulated his skipper. "It will save our sticks for us yet."

Captain Warfield shook his head dubiously.

The sea on the lagoon went swiftly down with the change of wind, but they were beginning to feel the heave and lift of the outer sea breaking across the atoll. There were not so many trees remaining. Some had been broken off, others uprooted. One tree they saw snap off halfway up and whirl away by the wind into the lagoon, three persons clinging to it. Two detached themselves and swam to the *Tahaa*. Not long after, just before darkness, they saw one jump overboard from that schooner's stern and strike out strongly for the *Malahini* through the white, spitting wavelets.

"It's Tai-Hotauri," was Grief's judgment. "Now we'll have the news."

The Kanaka caught the bobstay, climbed over the bow, and crawled aft. Time was given him to breathe, and then, behind the partial shelter of the cabin, in broken snatches and largely by signs, he told his story.

"Narii . . . damn robber . . . He want steal . . . pearls . . . kill Parlay . . . One man kill Parlay . . . no man know what man . . . Three Kanakas, Narii, me . . . five beans . . . hat . . . Narii say one bean black . . . nobody know . . . Narii damn liar . . . all beans black . . . copra-shed dark . . . every man get black bean . . . Big wind come . . . no chance . . . Everybody get up tree . . . No good luck them pearls, I tell you before . . . no good luck."

"Where's Parlay?" Grief shouted.

"Up tree . . . Three of his Kanakas same tree. Narii and one Kanaka 'nother tree . . . My tree blow to hell, then I come on board."

"Where's the pearls?"

"Up tree along Parlay. Mebbe Narii get them pearl yet."

In the ear of one after another Grief passed on Tai-Hotauri's story. Captain Warfield was particularly incensed, and they could see him grinding his teeth.

Hermann went below and returned with a riding light, but the moment it was lifted above the level of the cabin wall the wind blew it out. He had better success with the binnacle lamp, which was lighted only after many collective attempts.

"A fine night of wind!" Grief yelled in Mulhall's ear. "And blowing harder all the time."

"How hard?"

"A hundred miles an hour . . . two hundred . . . I don't know. . . . Harder than *I've* ever seen it."

The lagoon grew more and more troubled by the sea that swept across the atoll. Hundreds of leagues of ocean was being backed up by the hurricane, which more than over came the lowering effect of the ebb tide. The moment the tide began to rise the increase in the size of the seas was noticeable. Moon and wind were heaping the South Pacific on Hikihoho atoll.

Captain Warfield returned from one of his periodical trips to the engine room with the word that the engineer lay in a faint.

"Can't let that engine stop!" he concluded helplessly.

"All right!" Grief said. "Bring him on deck. I'll spell him."

The hatch to the engine room being battened down, access was gained through a narrow passage from the cabin. The heat and gas fumes were stifling. Grief took one hasty, comprehensive examination of the engine and the fittings of the

tiny room, then blew out the oil lamp. After that he worked
in darkness, save for the glow from endless cigars which he
went into the cabin to light. Even-tempered as he was, he
soon began to give evidences of the strain of being pent up
with a mechanical monster that toiled, sobbed, and slubbered
in the shouting dark. Naked to the waist, covered with grease
and oil, bruised and skinned from being knocked about by the
plunging, jumping vessel, his head swimming from the
mixture of gas and air he was compelled to breathe, he
labored on hour after hour, petting, blessing, nursing, and
cursing the engine and all its parts. The ignition began to go
bad. The feed grew worse. Worst of all, the cylinders began to
heat. In a consultation held in the cabin, the half-caste
engineer begged and pleaded to stop the engine for half
an hour in order to cool it and attend to the water circulation. Captain Warfield was against stopping. The half-caste
swore that the engine would ruin itself and stop anyway and
for good. Grief, greasy and battered, with glaring eyes, yelled
and cursed them both down and issued commands. Mulhall,
the supercargo, and Hermann were set to work in the cabin
double- and triple-straining the gasoline. A hole was chopped
through the engine room floor, and a Kanaka heaved bilge
water over the cylinders, while Grief continued to souse
running parts in oil.

"Didn't know you were a gasoline expert," Captain Warfield admired when Grief came into the cabin to catch a
breath of little less impure air.

"I bathe in gasoline," he grated savagely through his teeth.
"I eat it."

What other uses he might have found for it were never
given, for at that moment all the men in the cabin, as well as

the gasoline being strained, were smashed for'ard against the bulkhead as the *Malahini* took an abrupt, deep dive. For the space of several minutes, unable to gain their feet, they rolled back and forth, pounded and hammered from wall to wall. The schooner, swept by three big seas, creaked and groaned and quivered, and from the weight of water on her decks behaved logily. Grief crept to the engine, while Captain Warfield waited his chance to get through the companion-way and out on deck.

It was half an hour before he came back.

"Whaleboat's gone!" he reported. "Galley's gone! Everything gone except the deck and hatches! And if that engine hadn't been going we'd be gone. Keep up the good work!"

By midnight the engineer's lungs and head had been sufficiently cleared of gas fumes to let him relieve Grief, who went on deck to get his own head and lungs clear. He joined the others crouched behind the cabin, holding on with their hands and made doubly secure by rope-lashings. It was a complicated huddle, for it was the only place of refuge for the Kanakas. Some of them had accepted the skipper's invitation into the cabin but had been driven out by the fumes. The *Malahini* was being plunged down and swept frequently, and what they breathed was air and spray and water commingled.

"Making heavy weather of it, Mulhall!" Grief shouted to his guest between immersions.

Mulhall, strangling and choking, could only nod. The scuppers could not carry off the burden of water on the schooner's deck. She rolled it out and took it in over one rail and the other; and at times, nose thrown skyward, sitting down on her heel, she avalanched it aft. It surged along the poop gangways, poured over the top of the cabin, submerging and bruising those that clung on, and went out over the stern-rail.

Mulhall saw him first, and drew Grief's attention. It was Narii Herring, crouching and holding on where the dim binnacle light shone upon him. He was quite naked, save for a belt and a bare-bladed knife thrust between it and the skin.

Captain Warfield untied his lashings and made his way over the bodies of the others. When his face became visible in the light from the binnacle it was working with anger. They could see him speak, but the wind tore the sound away. He would not put his lips to Narii's ear. Instead, he pointed over the side. Narii Herring understood. His white teeth showed in an amused and sneering smile, and he stood up, a magnificent figure of a man.

"It's murder!" Mulhall yelled to Grief.

"He'd have murdered Old Parlay!" Grief yelled back.

For the moment the poop was clear of water and the *Malahini* on an even keel. Narii made a bravado attempt to walk to the rail, but was flung down by the wind. Thereafter he crawled, disappearing in the darkness, and all were sure he had gone over the side. The *Malahini* dived deep, and when they emerged from the flood that swept aft, Grief got Mulhall's ear.

"Don't worry! Can't lose *him*! He's the Fish Man of Tahiti! He'll cross the lagoon and land on the other rim of the atoll if there's any atoll left!"

Five minutes afterward, in another submergence, a mess of bodies poured down on them over the top of the cabin.

These they seized and held till the water cleared, when they carried them below and learned their identity. Old Parlay lay on his back on the floor, with closed eyes and without movement. The other two were his Kanaka cousins. All three were naked and bloody. The arm of one Kanaka hung helpless and broken at his side. The other man bled freely from a hideous scalp wound.

"Narii did that?" Mulhall demanded.

Grief shook his head. "No; it's from being smashed along the deck and over the house!"

Something suddenly ceased, leaving them in dizzying uncertainty. For the moment it was hard to realize there was no wind. With the absolute abruptness of a sword slash, the wind had been chopped off. The schooner rolled and plunged, fetching up on her anchors with a crash which for the first time they could hear. Also, for the first time they could hear the water washing about on deck. The engineer threw off the propeller and eased the engine down.

"We're in the dead center," Grief said. "Now for the shift. It will come as hard as ever." He looked at the barometer. "29.32," he read.

Not in a moment could he tone down the voice which for hours had battled against the wind, and so loudly did he speak that in the quiet it hurt the others' ears.

"All his ribs are smashed," the supercargo said, feeling along Parlay's side. "He's still breathing, but he's a goner."

Old Parlay groaned, moved one arm impotently, and opened his eyes. In them was the light of recognition.

"My brave gentlemen," he whispered haltingly. "Don't forget . . . the auction . . . at ten o'clock . . . in hell."

His eyes dropped shut and the lower jaw threatened to

drop, but he mastered the qualms of dissolution long enough to emit one final, loud, derisive cackle.

Above and below pandemonium broke out. The old familiar roar of the wind was with them. The *Malahini*, caught broadside, was pressed down almost on her beam ends as she swung the arc compelled by her anchors. They rounded her into the wind, where she jerked to an even keel. The propeller was thrown on, and the engine took up its work again.

"Northwest!" Captain Warfield shouted to Grief when he came on deck. "Hauled eight points like a shot!"

"Narii'll never get across the lagoon now!" Grief observed.

"Then he'll blow back to our side, worse luck!"

After the passing of the center the barometer began to rise. Equally rapid was the fall of the wind. When it was no more than a howling gale, the engine lifted up in the air, parted its bed-plates with a last convulsive effort of its forty horsepower, and lay down on its side. A wash of water from the bilge sizzled over it and the steam arose in clouds. The engineer wailed his dismay, but Grief glanced over the wreck affectionately and went into the cabin to swab the grease off his chest and arms with bunches of cotton waste.

The sun was up and the gentlest of summer breezes blowing when he came on deck, after sewing up the scalp of one Kanaka and setting the other's arm. The *Malahini* lay close in to the beach. For'ard, Hermann and the crew were heaving in and straightening out the tangle of anchors. The *Papara* and the *Tahaa* were gone, and Captain Warfield, through the glasses, was searching the opposite rim of the atoll.

"Not a stick left of them," he said. "That's what comes of not having engines. They must have dragged across before the big shift came."

Ashore, where Parlay's house had been, was no vestige of any house. For the space of three hundred yards, where the sea had breached, no tree or even stump was left. Here and there, farther along, stood an occasional palm, and there were many which had been snapped off above the ground. In the crown of one surviving palm Tai-Hotauri asserted he saw something move. There were no boats left to the *Malahini*, and they watched him swim ashore and climb the tree.

When he came back, they helped over the rail a young native girl of Parlay's household. But first she passed up to them a battered basket. In it was a litter of blind kittens—all dead save one that feebly mewed and staggered on awkward legs.

"Hello!" said Mulhall. "Who's that?"

Along the beach they saw a man walking. He moved casually, as if out for a morning stroll. Captain Warfield gritted his teeth. It was Narii Herring.

"Hello, skipper!" Narii called, when he was abreast of them. "Can I come aboard and get some breakfast?"

Captain Warfield's face and neck began to swell and turn purple. He tried to speak, but choked.

"For two cents—for two cents——" was all he could manage to articulate.